THE SECRET CIRCLE
OF IMAGINARY FRIENDS

THE SECRET CIRCLE
OF IMAGINARY FRIENDS

MIKE JEAVONS

For Gracie

CHAPTER ONE

'Okay, okay,' said Amie from the other side of the bedroom door. 'But you have to be quiet. We can't wake up Mum and Dad.'

Simon rubbed his sore eyes and propped himself up onto his elbows. He glanced over at the dull red glow of the alarm clock on his bedside table and could just make out that it was almost two o'clock in the morning.

Simon was often kept awake at night by the sound of his sister muttering quietly in her bedroom. His parents thought that Amie had an imaginary friend; after all, a lot of seven-year-old girls did. They assumed it would be something that she would grow out of, but she had been doing it almost every night for the past three weeks, and would often keep Simon awake until way after midnight.

'Amie, please,' said Simon.

It seemed that she hadn't heard him, as her soft but squeaky footsteps on the old floorboards outside his bedroom still lead down the hallway toward the stairs. Simon expected his parents to burst through their own door at any moment and demand to know why she was out of bed. A few more groans of the floorboards later, they still hadn't come, and Simon could tell that his sister was halfway down the stairs and almost inside the kitchen.

Simon tried to ignore the big-brotherly thoughts inside him, but knew that he couldn't. He kicked off the bed sheets and forced himself to his feet.

He trudged sleepily across his bedroom and carefully pulled the door a little less than halfway open, just so it didn't make that loud 'click' that it always did, and slipped through into the dark hallway.

Simon knew where all the squeaky floorboards were, so he picked his steps lightly as he made his way silently along the hallway and down the stairs. The kitchen was blanketed in the dim moonlight which washed in through the large window but, even with the light, Simon couldn't see his sister.

'Amie?' he said.

Simon walked around the small breakfast table in the centre of the room and poked his head into the dining room.

'Are you in here?'

A reply came in the form of the front door creaking at the other side of the house.

Simon moved back across the kitchen and through the door which led into the hallway. The front door was wide open, and a wash of yellow light poured in from a nearby lamppost.

Outside, Simon could just see the top of Amie's head over the hedge at the other end of the front garden. He slipped on his trainers, grabbed his jacket and followed her.

The night was cool, and there was a frosty breeze making the trees dance along the side of the narrow pavement. Simon and his family lived in a small village outside the big towns and cities so, rather than lots of tall buildings and blaring traffic, his house and the few others around it were surrounded by miles of grass, farmers' fields, and dense, tangled woodland. This made it extra quiet at night, with the only sounds being the light splashing off the stream which ran alongside the road and the occasional hoot from a distant owl.

Simon scanned the village green and noticed a dainty shadow pass along a wooden fence. The shadow shrank as the fence stopped at the entrance to an alleyway.

Where was she going? Simon felt a knot forming in his stomach. His sister was heading away from the light of the lampposts and was quickly vanishing into the black of the night. He was desperate not to follow; he would have given anything to just turn around, ignore what was happening and hide in the warmth of his bed.

He didn't know why he didn't just call to her and demand that she follow him home. It was the curious side of him which had taken over, and he desperately wanted to know why his seven-year-old sister was sneaking out in the middle of the night.

Simon jogged across the village green and hurried through the alley. Even he didn't like passing through the alley at night, and he was twelve, so he had no idea how Amie could do it alone.

Simon slipped out from the alley and kept himself in the shadows. There were no lampposts at the edge of the village; the only thing which lit his path was the dull white glow of the moon.

Amie followed the winding path at the back of a line of thatched roof houses. To the left was a grassy bank which led up to a wall of tall, leafless trees. She was holding her left hand up so that it was level with her head, and Simon could tell that she was holding one of her stuffed animals tight against her chest. The frills at the bottom of her blue nightgown were dragging along the dirt path; her slippers were wet and brown with muck.

Amie turned left as the path wound up the bank and into the trees. Normally, Simon was certain that his sister wouldn't go anywhere near the woods, but here she was,

4

heading into the trees without even looking back.

Simon definitely didn't want to follow now. He spent a lot of time in the woods with his friends, but that was always during the day; he had never been inside those trees during the dark, especially not at two o'clock in the morning. But it was too late to turn back now; Amie had gone into the woods, so now he had to as well.

It was even darker within the trees. There was a ceiling of tangled branches which stopped all but a few trickles of moonlight from squeezing through, and there was a crunchy carpet of leaves littered across the hard ground.

Simon could just make out his sister between the thick trunks of the black trees. She would drift in and out of darkness, passing through the streams of moonlight, and she left small tracks along the ground where she was obviously shuffling her feet through the leaves.

Somewhere deeper in the darkness an animal barked. It brought the knot in Simon's stomach up into his throat, and he even felt his drumming heart stop so he could listen. It sounded a lot like a fox, but it could have been a dog. Whatever it was, it was close.

Ahead, a distant yellow glow rose from the ground, which seemed to brighten with each step Simon made. As Amie passed in front of the light it outlined her tiny frame.

There was another high-pitched bark from behind.

Simon ducked behind a thick fallen branch and pressed his back tight against it. He looked out through the maze of twisted trees, his eyes searching for any signs of movement. There was nothing, which was what he had hoped for.

Simon turned and looked out over the top of the fallen branch. The moon must have crept behind a cloud, because the darkness swelled all around and the small straggles of white light disappeared. The only sign of light was the dull yellow glow from deeper within the trees.

Simon had completely lost sight of his sister. He shot up and leapt over the fallen branch. He bolted toward the yellow light, but didn't get far before he tripped on a tree root and hit the ground with an explosion of leaves.

'Amie!' Simon cried.

He listened for a moment, but no reply came.

'Amie, can you hear me?'

Simon scrambled back to his feet and pelted in the direction of the yellow glow, cracking into the trunks of the trees as he struggled to see ahead.

'Amie, where are you?' he called.

Still, no response came from within the darkness.

Simon stopped and yelled as loud as his lungs would let him. 'AMIE!'

He could feel his heart hammering against the inside of his chest and, despite the cold, sweat ran down his forehead. Footsteps scurried through the leaves somewhere behind and Simon spun on the spot. There was another crunching of leaves from the left, then again from behind. Footsteps scurried all around, but the only thing Simon could see was the darkness.

'AMIE!' he screamed and he spun around once more.

'What?' said Amie, who stood looking up at her brother with her stuffed bear still held tight to her chest.

CHAPTER TWO

During the entire walk home Amie refused to give any reason as to where she was going. The yellow glow had gone, but the streaks of moonlight had returned to light the path home.

'Why were you following me?' said Amie.

'Does it matter? Why are you here, anyway?'

Amie said nothing; she just allowed her brother to pull her by the arm out of the woods.

'Do you know how dangerous it is?'

'It's fine,' she said.

'It's not fine. Imagine if an animal found you, or some weird old bloke or something.'

'It's safe.'

'Don't be ridiculous! Of course it isn't safe!'

'I couldn't help it. I was sleepwalking.'

'Mum and Dad might think you're sleepwalking, but

you're not, are you?'

Amie scrunched up her nose and squealed as she stumbled.

'Stop pulling me so hard.'

This time Simon didn't speak. He led his sister through the alley between the houses and back across the village green.

'You better hope Mum and Dad aren't awake,' he grunted.

'I'm not going to be the one getting into trouble. You followed me.'

'And you were the one who went out in the first place. I couldn't just let you wander off without doing something.'

As they turned in through the front gate and headed down the garden path to the front door, which still hung open, the frantic figure of their mother leapt out.

'WHAT ON EARTH ARE YOU DOING?'

***

Simon had been allowed back to bed just as the clock flashed three o'clock. His eyes were sore and his head was throbbing from the tongue-lashing his mum and dad had given him. He had been forced to sit and explain everything that had happened and then listen as his dad told him why all of that had been wrong and that he should have woken them up as soon as he knew Amie was out of bed.

Amie, however, had been ordered straight to bed. Simon could hear her muttering quietly as he buried himself in his bedcovers and fell instantly to sleep.

***

The next morning Simon struggled to pull himself out of his deep, comfortable sleep. His mum had burst into his bedroom with ten minutes to go before he had to leave the house and head to school.

'Five more minutes,' he groaned.

'You've had thirty-five! Up!'

Simon rolled out from the warmth beneath his covers and washed and dressed in record time. As he appeared at the bottom of the stairs his mum waved him towards the front door with a piece of buttered toast.

'Come on, we needed to be in the car two minutes ago.'

'Have you seen my tie?' said Simon as he slipped on his shoes.

'Last place I saw it was round your neck.'

'I've looked there.'

'Very funny. You'll have to do without today. Out.'

It was a very bright October morning, but there was an icy chill still hanging from the night before. Simon zipped his jacket up to his chin and climbed into the back of his Mum's dark green car, where Amie sat waiting.

'You're going to make us late,' she said.

'Well, you're the reason I woke up late in the first place.'

'I didn't ask you to follow me.'

'I told you why. Plus, you haven't told me why you were really there.'

'I did; I was sleep-walking.'

'Don't lie to me. I heard you talking.'

'Sleep-talking.'

Simon shook his head as his mum climbed into the driver's seat and started the engine.

'Cutting it rather fine this morning, kids,' she said.

The village of Hedgely, where they lived, had very little to see or do. There was a pub, a post office, and a village hall but, apart from that, there was nothing of any interest. Every morning they had to travel to the neighbouring village so they could go to school. The nearest supermarket was in the next town and if they ever wanted to do something fun, like go to the cinema, they had to go even further than that. It wasn't easy living in the middle of the countryside in a village where everybody knew everybody else's business, but that's the way their parents preferred it. They both worked in the centre of a big town, so they didn't see any need in living there as well.

The drive to school took ten minutes through the narrow country roads. Sometimes it would take less time, but they would usually get stuck behind a tractor which rumbled deeply as it trundled slowly along. That morning they got stuck behind two.

As they pulled up to the old iron school gates, Simon and Amie bolted from the car and across the playground as the morning bell signalled the start of first period. Simon left his sister behind as he burst through the double doors and ran down the empty corridor, his footsteps echoing loudly. The school building itself was old; everything was painted in shades of beige and it was always chilly, even in the summer.

Simon turned a corner and stopped outside room 7B. He peered in through the small window in the door and saw his empty desk in the middle of the room. Mrs Ramsworth was calling out the morning register, her eyes peering over her thin glasses.

Simon tried to open the door quietly but it groaned like an ancient piece of machinery. The whole class looked his way except for Mrs Ramsworth.

'Good morning, Mr Andrews, nice of you to join us,' she said.

'Sorry.'

'Sorry, what?'

'Sorry, Mrs Ramsworth.'

'Becoming a habit, it seems. Sit down.'

Simon slipped between the desks and sat in his regular seat beside Jonathon Turner, a short, plump boy with messy black hair. He smirked as Simon took his pencil case out of his bag. Mrs Ramsworth finished calling out the register and began scribbling some words on the blackboard.

'Great, more spelling,' muttered Simon.

'Mm,' said Jonathon. He had his head resting on his upright arm.

'What's wrong with you?'

'Oh, nothing,' he said as he fought back a yawn.

'You look more tired than me. Your eyes are red.'

'No, no, I'm all right.'

'Boys,' snapped Mrs Ramsworth. 'Talking will be done at break time. I have a list of words on the board which I want you all to copy into your workbooks. We're getting to the hard stuff now, which you'll need when we start looking into eighteenth century poetry.'

There were a few groans around the class, which Mrs Ramsworth tried to ignore.

'So get started, you've got two minutes before we move on. Miss Walker!'

The whole class turned to look at Rebecca Walker, who had shot up in her seat.

'Yes, Miss!' she yelped.

'Do you really think it is appropriate for you to be sleeping in my class? Go to the Headmaster's office immediately.'

Rebecca slipped from the classroom against the snickering of her classmates. Simon turned back to look at Jonathon, who was still resting his head on his hand.

'Hey,' said Simon. 'You're going to end up like Becky if you're not careful.'

'Mm,' mumbled Jonathon.

Simon gave him a jab in the side with his elbow.

'What?'

'Why are you so tired?'

'I'm not.'

'At least I have a good excuse; I was up until about three o'clock. What were you doing last night?'

'Nothing.'

'What time did you go to bed?'

'I don't know. Eight or something.'

'Last night or this morning?'

Jonathon grunted.

'Gentlemen,' said Mrs Ramsworth. 'I didn't plan on breaking any records for the number of people to be sent to Mr Cricklewood's office, but I'm quite happy to if you don't stop talking.'

Will, a tall boy who sat at the front of the class, yawned loudly.

'Apparently today is a day for trying my patience. Mr Graves, go and join Miss Walker immediately!'

That's how the lessons went that morning. Three people were sent out of Mrs Ramsworth's lessons for falling asleep in class, much to everybody else's amusement. Their snorts of laughter then had two boys at the back of the room sent out, and when everybody else began talking about it, Mrs Ramsworth asked the Head teacher to come and talk to the class. He had been in class for ten minutes, repeating the importance of paying attention and listening, before Jonathon grunted a loud snore. Mr Cricklewood was known to sometimes get red-faced when he was angry, but Simon had never seen his face get quite *that* red. His head looked like a giant tomato with beady eyes and a grey wig. Simon wasn't even sure that his ranting had even made sense; it sounded more like an angry list of vicious words.

During the lesson the only thing Simon learnt was that Mr Cricklewood had surprisingly minty breath. When the bell rang, those who had managed to remain in class packed away their pencil cases and workbooks and managed to stifle their laughter until they were out in the safety of the corridor.

Next was maths. Even on a good day Simon found it difficult to stay awake listening to the teacher drone on about equations and remainders. Only one person was caught sleeping, but Simon knew others had managed to have a quick nap.

At lunchtime the entire school was forced to spend the hour outside while being overlooked by a glowering Mr Cricklewood. The air was bitter and some pupils were complaining that they couldn't feel their ears ('Why would you need to feel your ears?' Mr Cricklewood had asked them), but everybody was just reminded that the bitter air would help wake them up. Stories spread quickly around the playground; it hadn't just been Simon's class to have sleepers sent from the room. Amie's class had a girl sent out, as well as two from the year above who Simon didn't really know.

Simon had been kicking a football around with his friends Abdul and David when he spotted Jonathon speaking to Becky Walker on a bench beside the mobile classroom. He jogged over to them and smiled, but they didn't smile back.

'What did Mr Cricklewood say?' asked Simon.

'He's writing a letter to our parents,' grumbled

Jonathon.

'He said if it happens again he'll call them and make them come in,' added Becky.

'So why are you all so tired?'

Jonathon shrugged. 'No reason.'

'What about you?'

'Same,' said Becky.

'There must be a reason. I had about four hours' sleep last night and I feel like nodding off, but I've managed to stop myself. You guys must have had even less than that.'

'It's nothing,' said Jonathon.

'It can't be nothing. You can't all be tired for nothing.'

'Well, we are.'

'You're all tired for the same reason?'

Jonathon shrugged.

'I'll tell you why I only had four hours' sleep,' said Simon. 'I was following my little sister in the woods. I've no idea why she was there, but she was.'

Jonathon and Becky exchanged glances.

'What happened?' said Becky.

'It's hard to say; it was dark. But there was a weird yellow light and some animals making sounds.'

'Did you see anything?' said Jonathon.

'No, it was too dark. Why?'

'No reason.'

'That's all you seem to say! There must be a reason!'

Jonathon stood up. 'There isn't, okay? I'm just tired, Becky is just tired, so stop asking all of these questions. I had enough with Mr Cricklewood; I don't need any more from you.'

'Okay, fine,' said Simon. He turned and ran back over to join Abdul and David.

CHAPTER THREE

That night Simon received another round of stern lectures from his parents about going outside after dark. He lost count of the amount of times he was told he should have woken them up instead of following his sister into the woods, and by the end, he was struggling to even concentrate on what they were saying. As the day had gone on Simon had started to realise just how tired his classmates must have felt. Twice during afternoon lessons he had nodded off only to wake up as his head slipped from its resting place on his upright hand.

Others hadn't been so lucky. Gossip had spread around the school that another three students had been sent to Mr Cricklewood's office. None of them would give a reason why they were all so tired.

What Simon couldn't understand was why his sister seemed unfazed by her lack of sleep. By eight o'clock that evening she was still bouncing on the spot holding her soft bear, its tattered face expressionless as she swung it around her head.

Simon, however, couldn't keep himself awake. He was slouched on the sofa, watching a film with the rest of his family. Despite a fast-paced car chase and thumping music, Simon couldn't keep his eyes open for more than a few seconds at a time.

'See, that's what you get for sneaking out,' said his dad.

Simon opened his eyes and saw the end credits rolling on the television; he had missed half of the film.

'Time for bed, kids,' his mum added.

'Oh, Mum,' said Amie.

Simon didn't argue. The thought of crawling into bed sounded like the best idea he had heard in a long time, so he headed sluggishly upstairs and brushed his teeth before trudging into his room. As he covered himself in the warmth beneath his bed sheets he closed his eyes and fell asleep straight away, despite the sound of his sister chatting away to herself in the room next door.

***

Simon felt something sweep against his face. He stirred but

didn't open his eyes, and brushed whatever it was away with a lazy swipe of an arm. It was warm and quiet – not time to wake up.

He felt it again. It wasn't something small, like a fly. It was something big, like a hand.

Simon opened his eyes but the room was cloaked in darkness, and it took his eyes a few seconds to adjust. He sat up and squinted. Everything was still except the beating of his heart.

I must have been dreaming, he thought, and he lay back down.

A creak outside his bedroom door made him sit up again. He held his breath so he could listen. There was another creak a little further down the corridor.

'Amie?' whispered Simon.

Another creak, this time closer to his sister's room.

'Amie, are you out of bed again?' he said a little more loudly.

There was no response, just another creak of the floorboards.

Simon rolled his eyes and threw the covers away. If Amie was out of bed again then he wanted to be sure that his parents knew about it. He pulled his bedroom door open slowly, being careful to stop just before it made the loud clicking sound, and he slipped out into the hallway.

There was a streak of moonlight pouring in through the window at the top of the stairs, which made it easier for Simon to see. His sister wasn't there, but her door was ajar.

'Amie?' he whispered.

There was no sound coming from her room. Simon chose his footsteps carefully and, avoiding the creakiest of the old floorboards, stepped towards his sister's bedroom door. He pushed it open and crept inside.

Amie's room was slightly smaller than Simon's, and she had so many stuffed animals that there was barely enough room left for herself. She would spend hours arranging them perfectly, keeping the stuffed lions away from the stuffed tigers and making sure the stuffed penguins had enough stuffed fish.

Simon stepped up to the bed, which was flat against the wall in the corner of the room. He could just make out the shape of his sister lying beneath the covers, moving gently as she breathed.

There was a ruffle of movement at the base of the bed. Simon stepped back and tried to keep himself as silent as possible; the last thing he wanted to do was wake up his sister and get caught out of bed. There was another ruffle along the bedcovers, but it was further down the bed, too far for his sister's little legs to reach. It was like there was something else there, maybe a toy, fidgeting about on top of the sheets.

But Simon couldn't see anything. Even though it was dark it was easy to see that there was nothing on Amie's bed, apart from Amie herself.

Then there was a thud on the floor. Simon gasped; had he knocked something?

There was a light breeze by Simon's feet and the door moved just an inch. The sound of creaking floorboards came fast and loud in the hallway. Simon could feel his heart again; it was hammering against the inside of his chest like an alarm bell.

He poked his head around the door and looked out into the moonlit hallway. The door to his parents' room was closed and the sound of the floorboards groaning loudly moved away toward the stairs. Simon followed, and moved along the hall and towards the kitchen.

There was a gentle rattle by the sink. The windowpane seemed to rumble gently, like a passing lorry had shaken the glass. A plate on the draining board clinked against a cup and the chair by the breakfast table scraped on the tiled floor.

Simon imagined a rat scurrying across the floor, or perhaps a cat had crept in and was darting between the shadows.

The back door opened and a cold blast of late night

23

breeze swept through the kitchen. Simon rounded the table and stood in the doorway. From there he could see over the back garden, from the brick patio at the front to the stepping stones which wound down to the tatty old shed at the back.

Was it a hedgehog, perhaps? Or maybe a badger. Simon saw a lot of badgers out in the country but had never heard of one running around a kitchen.

Simon stepped out into the garden and loudly cleared his throat. There was a rustle in the bushes by the shed.

The garden was suddenly lit up in a wash of yellow light. Simon spun on the spot to see his parents' bedroom light had turned on, which meant one of his parents was getting out of bed. Ignoring the twitching bush, Simon darted back into the kitchen, being as careful as possible not to make a sound as he closed the door. Heavy footsteps were treading on the creaky floorboards; someone was heading downstairs into the kitchen.

Simon snatched at a glass from the draining board and turned on the tap.

'Simon,' said his mum as she appeared in the kitchen. 'What are you doing?'

'Just getting a drink,' he said calmly.

CHAPTER FOUR

The next day Simon spent the early part of the morning playing video games with his dad. Their favourite game to play was football; Simon would pride himself on beating his dad almost every time they played, and this morning was no different. His dad was headed to London for two nights on business, so Simon was keen to get in some victories before he left.

'Cheater!' yelled his dad as Simon scored another goal.

Simon laughed. 'Two-nil!'

'You know some moves that you're not telling me. What do you press to do that thing?'

'What thing?'

'That thing where you spin around.'

'I don't know what thing you mean!'

That's how most of their conversations went while

they played, and it wound up Simon's mum to hear them bicker.

'You two are unbelievable!' she would say.

'You two are unbelievable!' Amie would repeat.

'Helen, tell your son to stop cheating,' his dad always said.

'Tell him yourself, Brian,' she would say back.

Helen tapped her watch and shot her husband a warning look. That meant playtime was over and it was time for Brian to leave for London.

After deciding that playing on his own wasn't particularly interesting, Simon slipped on his trainers and headed outside. Hedgely was surprisingly quiet for mid-morning on a Saturday. It was cold out, but that didn't usually stop the other children who lived in the village from gathering on the green to play cricket or take part in a hectic water fight. There weren't even any adults out; at this time of year it would be common to see people raking leaves from garden paths or giving their hedgerows one last trim before winter.

Simon crossed the green and headed into a small cul-de-sac where his friend Ryan lived. Ryan was in the year below Simon, but they went to the same school and would usually play football at lunchtime with David, Abdul, and Jonathon.

'He's in bed,' said Rachel, Ryan's older sister.

'Do you know when he'll be up?' asked Simon.

Rachel rolled her eyes. 'No.'

Rachel was very popular with the boys in Hedgely. She was a slim girl with straight blonde hair and extremely pretty features but, because she was sixteen, she never had any patience for Ryan or his friends. She was chewing gum loudly as she leaned against the wooden doorframe.

'Well, when he gets up, will you tell him I came round?'

'Will do,' she said.

Abdul and David didn't live in Hedgely, but Simon still had others he could call on. He made his way to the next road along, where Jonathon lived. His parents had moved away the year before to work in America, but Jonathon hadn't wanted to go, so he had moved to Hedgely to live with his grandma. They lived in a small bungalow close to the edge of the woodland on the outskirts of the village.

'I'm sorry, but Jonathon won't be coming out today,' said Mrs Turner, Jonathon's grandma. She was a large lady with white, wiry hair and a face marked with deep wrinkles. She peered over her round glasses while she spoke.

'How come?'

'No doubt he told you about being sent to the headmaster's office at school?' she said. 'If that wasn't enough, I caught him sneaking out of his room in the middle of the night!'

'Grandma!' said Jonathon from somewhere inside.

'Don't speak to me like that, young man.'

'Sorry, Grandma.'

'I should think so too. Do you want to be grounded for even longer?'

'No!'

Simon quickly grew bored of listening to their argument, so he made his excuses and left. He crossed the village green again and hopped over the stream, hoping his next attempt would be more successful.

It wasn't.

'I'm too tired,' said Will, a boy who was usually so full of energy he was difficult to keep still.

Simon didn't argue.

He wandered back to the village green, kicking a conker along the way. Why was everybody still so tired? And why had Jonathon been trying to sneak out? It reminded him of his sister and her journey through the woods in the middle of the night. The more he tried to make sense of everything, the less sense everything made. Why did everybody seem to be a part of something, but not him?

Simon sat on an old wooden bench at the edge of the village green and dug his heels into the soft earth. After sitting quietly with his thoughts for a moment, he felt the bench move as if somebody had sat next to him. Looking around, he was still very much alone; only the distant chirp of a bird was there to keep him company.

The bench dipped again, and the wood creaked slightly. Something caught Simon's eye and he leaned in for a better look.

He was sure it hadn't been there as he sat down. He hoped it had been, but he could have sworn it hadn't. Carved into the wood beside him were two words: *Stop Searching.*

CHAPTER FIVE

After dinner, as Simon sat watching Saturday night television with Amie and his mum, he kept his usual thoughts ('this is rubbish!') to himself and sat mulling over what had been happening. The more he thought about things, the more frustrated he became. There were so many questions swirling around in his mind that he had given himself a headache. At nine o'clock he went to bed and stared at the ceiling till his thoughts slowed down enough for him to ignore them and fall asleep.

Simon felt like he'd only been asleep for five minutes when he was awakened by the creaking floorboards outside his bedroom door. According to the clock it was almost three o'clock in the morning.

'Amie?' he said.

The floorboards creaked and groaned again as someone moved toward the stairs.

'Amie?'

'No,' came a hoarse reply from the hallway.

'What are you doing?' he said. Simon definitely didn't recognise the voice to be that of his sister.

There was no answer.

'Amie, what are you doing?'

'Shhhh.'

'Hey, no,' said Simon. He scrambled out of bed and moved over to the door. 'Get back to bed, now.'

A hoarse voice chuckled back at him. 'No.'

Simon poked his head through the doorway, but the hallway was empty.

'Amie?'

There was another snort of laughter from somewhere on the stairs.

'What are you doing?'

Simon crept out of his room and along the hallway. He leant over the banister at the top of the stairs and peered down. 'Amie?'

A chair in the kitchen was nudged.

Simon made his way downstairs and into the kitchen. His sister wasn't there, but a click from out by the living room drew his attention. A cool breeze filled the room and Simon knew that the front door was open.

'Amie, no!' said Simon in the quietest shout he

could manage. He bolted through to the hallway and out into the front garden.

'This isn't funny,' he said. 'Where are you?'

There was silence throughout Hedgely. Even the animals of the night were not calling out.

Looking out over the village green, Simon could see no sign of his sister.

'Amie?' he yelled, just as the front door slammed shut. He ran back and tugged on the handle, but the door had been locked from the inside.

'This isn't funny, let me in!'

There was no reply from inside.

Simon suddenly realised his bare feet were frozen on the cold stone path. His pyjamas were hardly suitable clothing to be wearing outside on an autumn night.

'Let me in!' he growled while fighting back the urge to bang on the door.

The sound of excited laughter came from further within the village.

Simon was sure he recognised it. He held his breath for a moment and listened.

There was another guffaw, this time louder, and Simon was sure he knew who it was. Despite his small size, Jonathon had a very recognisable laugh. It was a deep, booming laugh, and it was echoing through the village.

Simon considered shouting back, but just as he drew in a breath he saw somebody emerge onto the village green from behind the post office.

It was Jonathon, but he wasn't alone.

It was Will. He was a lot taller and thinner than Jonathon and was trudging sleepily behind.

But the third person to come out from behind the post office was someone Simon didn't recognise at all. He was tall and gangly and his back was hunched forward. Simon could see that if he stood at full height he would be as tall as an adult. He was making strange noises which sounded a bit like an angry horse, which Jonathon found so funny he had to stop and hold his waist so he could catch his breath. The trio were cutting across the green and heading toward the woodland which backed onto the village. It was the same way Amie had gone two nights before.

Simon looked back at the house. The door was still shut and there was no sign of movement from inside. He could see his bedroom window above. There was no light coming through the curtains, which meant his parents were still in bed.

He knew he shouldn't, but curiosity had taken over his senses. Simon headed out across the village green, his bare feet leaving tracks in the cold, damp grass.

CHAPTER SIX

Simon had followed Jonathon, Will, and the strange lanky boy through the village without being noticed. They made their way up the dirt path which cut through the grassy bank and disappeared inside the trees.

As he entered the woods Simon chose his footsteps carefully. The ground was littered with crunchy leaves and branches which had fallen from above and had created a noisy, brown carpet. He could see the others ahead, Jonathon still guffawing at the tall boy's funny noises.

Simon winced as he stepped onto something sharp. He grabbed the rough bark of a tree and bit his bottom lip till the pain passed. Perhaps heading into the woods with bare feet wasn't a smart move, but he had come too far now, and he couldn't turn back without first finding out what was going on.

Ahead, beyond the trio, was the dull yellow light

which Simon had seen two nights before. It was lighting the woodland in an eerie glow and was dancing against the thick tree trunks.

Somewhere an owl hooted, and Simon saw the tall boy stop and look around. Simon pressed himself up tightly to a tree and held his breath. He could feel his heart beating hard and his feet were numb from the cold. He allowed himself to breathe as the tall boy carried on walking towards the yellow light.

The glow brightened as Simon approached and, finally, he could tell what it was. A fire was burning somewhere further within the woodland. It crackled and popped softly, and the smell of scorched wood had drifted his way.

Jonathon, Will and the tall boy had stopped moving forward. Simon could see them ahead, standing together and talking. The yellow glow had scatterings of orange filtering through and Simon could better make out their surroundings. They stood in a wide, round clearing which surrounded the large bonfire. Around the fire were tree stumps placed several paces apart from each other. The ground between them had been cleared of fallen autumn leaves.

'Hey,' came a soft voice Simon didn't recognise.

The trio turned to face the fire and Simon saw the

small figure of a girl come out from behind the flames.

'Hi, Claire,' said Will.

Simon didn't know anybody called Claire and he didn't know that Will did either.

'Hi, Hemlin,' said Claire. The lanky boy waved back.

Simon definitely didn't know anybody called Hemlin.

'Are we the first here?' said Jonathon.

'Yes, we've been waiting ages,' said another boy who darted out from behind the fire. He had a high-pitched, nasal voice and was breathing loudly.

'Hey, Lothgar,' said Will. 'Didn't know you were hiding there.'

'What time is it?' asked Jonathon.

'Almost twenty past three,' said the girl known as Claire. 'Nearly time.'

'Guys!' came a loud voice from behind. Simon recognised it to be Ryan's.

'Ryan!' called Jonathon.

Simon managed to duck down behind a fallen tree trunk just as Ryan, a tall boy with short brown hair, darted past. He was being followed by a shorter fat boy who seemed to drag his hands along the ground like a monkey.

'How are you, Thump?' said Claire.

'I'm fine,' said Thump. 'But I think you should

know there is a boy outside the circle watching us.'

Simon felt his stomach drop as everyone standing around the campfire turned and looked his way. He didn't think about what he should do next; he just turned and ran as fast as his bloodied, aching feet would allow. It was hard to see ahead but Simon fought to keep his balance as his shins smacked into tree stumps and fallen branches. He could tell there were others following and he was sure they were getting nearer, but he dared not look back.

Simon burst out from the woods and scrambled down the bank. His legs were throbbing from the pain. He bolted through the alley and out onto the village green, the others' footsteps even closer behind. He veered left and crossed the small wooden bridge which arched across the stream, then crossed the road and grabbed the fencepost to help steer him into his front garden.

The front door was open. As he bolted inside Simon flung the door shut but he didn't hear a bang. He headed upstairs, only half-heartedly trying to miss the noisy steps, and threw open his bedroom door, which swung out with a loud crack.

'Okay, so you didn't stop searching' said the thin, olive-skinned creature sitting on Simon's bed. 'So I guess we might as well let you in on our little secret.'

CHAPTER SEVEN

Simon held his breath and blinked. His eyes must have been playing some kind of trick on him.

'Are you going to just stand there, or are you going to sit down so we can talk?' said the creature.

'I, err…' Simon trailed off a sentence he didn't even mean to start. On his bed, with its bony legs crossed, was a scrawny, leathery-skinned creature with a large head and round, glassy eyes. It had a mouth full of needle-sharp teeth upturned into a wry smile.

'What's the matter?' said the creature. Its voice seemed nasal and forced, like something was blocking its small, upturned nose.

'Who- what are you?' uttered Simon.

'I'm a part of what you've been looking for,' it replied.

'What do you mean?'

The creature chuckled. 'I think maybe you should sit down. Your feet look rather sore.'

Simon looked down at his feet and saw them brown and red from dirt and blood. They felt like he'd been walking on hot glass, so he did as the creature said and perched on the edge of his bed. He had left a trail of black footprints across the cream carpet and he couldn't help but worry about what his parents would say.

'Don't worry about the mess,' said the creature. 'We'll make sure it's all clean for when your mother and father wake up.'

'We...?' said Simon as a stumpy little creature waddled into his room. It had yellowish skin and a glum face which hung down like it had melted. It started scrubbing the floor with a damp cloth and was mumbling quietly to itself.

'I...' Simon was struggling to finish a sentence.

'I realise you probably have a lot of questions. People always do when they first see us and it's natural to have them, of course. But let me try to explain it to you as best as I can.' The creature sat back on the bed and nestled into Simon's pillow. 'My name is Kannon and I am your imaginary friend.'

'Imaginary?' said Simon. 'You mean, you're just... in my mind?'

'Not exactly,' said the creature known as Kannon.

'If I were, you certainly wouldn't be able to feel this.' Kannon clicked two of his long, bony fingers and the stumpy creature toddled over to Simon and began wiping his feet with another cloth.

Simon winced. 'Ouch.'

'We're not imaginary to you,' said Kannon. 'But we must be to everybody else. The most important thing you must know, and it is vital that you remember, is that the adults can never know about us.'

'Why not?' said Simon.

'Because if they knew that we were real they would capture us and take us away.' Kannon sneered and thumped his balled-up fist into the bedcovers.

Simon's feet stung as the small creature wiped away the mud, but already they felt much cleaner and the pain had started to dull.

'So, who does know about you?'

'Only members of the Secret Circle can know about us. There are others, like you, who we have showed ourselves to.'

'The people in the woods?' said Simon.

'That's right,' said Kannon. 'Some of them I believe are your friends. It is only they who know the truth, and that is how it must remain. We didn't intend on revealing ourselves to you and, had it not been for your persistence, we wouldn't have had to. We were quite happy with keeping it with your sister.'

Suddenly a flurry of Simon's questions had been answered. Amie's visits to the woods, her talking to herself at night – it had all been because of her imaginary friend, who just happened to be real.

'But my parents know that Amie has an imaginary friend. They think it's just a phase she's going through,' said Simon.

'Exactly,' said Kannon with a nod of his oversized head. 'They don't know that we're real, so your sister has done as we asked. She is a good girl, that one.'

Simon pulled back his left foot as a sharp pain shot through his ankle. The stumpy creature grunted, clearly annoyed that his cleaning duty had been interrupted.

'Are things any clearer now?'

Simon thought for a few moments. 'Not really,' he said. 'I understand that you're secret, we can't talk about you to anybody who doesn't already know about you, but what I don't understand is why.'

'Why? Well, isn't a childhood supposed to be fun? We just help with the fun, that's all.'

'Where do you come from?'

Kannon smiled. 'Your imagination, of course.'

The stumpy creature grumbled and returned to

scrubbing the carpet. Simon wiggled his toes and admired his clean, though still bruised and scratched, feet.

'It's all just so hard to believe,' said Simon. 'I mean… I had a hundred things in my head as to why Amie was sneaking out at night, but none of them came even close to this.'

'Then you don't use your imagination enough,' said Kannon as his expression darkened.

'But this isn't my imagination,' said Simon, unaware that he had raised his voice. 'This is all happening. I'm not asleep; you're right here.'

Simon reached out his hand to touch Kannon, but the creature lurched back and turned up his nose.

'You're not taking this as well as the others,' muttered Kannon.

'Can you blame me?' blurted Simon. 'You're here telling me that you're imaginary, that I can't talk to anybody else about you, but my friends can see you as well. It feels like I've gone mad.'

'Maybe you have.'

'Maybe I have!'

Simon heard a thud from somewhere outside his room. Footsteps thundered across the floor and the door to his parents' bedroom swung open. A moment later the groggy figure of his mum was silhouetted in the doorway.

'Simon, what are you doing?' she croaked.

Simon glanced at an empty space on his bed where Kannon had been. The stumpy creature on the floor had also disappeared. 'Nothing,' he said.

'Why are you out of bed?'

'I had a nightmare,' said Simon.

'Right, well, get back into bed. It's nearly five o'clock, you have school in the morning, and I'm supposed to be in work early.'

'Okay, Mum, sorry.'

Once his mum had left, Simon kicked his legs under the covers and laid flat on his bed. He couldn't sleep. Not that he was trying – he just stared silently at the ceiling and tried to come to terms with what had just happened.

'Believe me yet?' said Kannon, who was suddenly once again sat crossed-legged at the bottom of the bed.

Simon sat up and strained to see the bony figure through the darkness. 'I don't know.'

'Well, I know what will help you make up your mind,' said Kannon.

'What?'

'Come with me and I'll introduce you to the rest of the Secret Circle.'

Simon thought for a second. 'Okay.'

CHAPTER EIGHT

Simon followed Kannon out of the house and into the woods at the back of the village. Lit only by the streams of moonlight which filtered through the branches above, they moved through the trees and Simon once again saw the glow of the fire.

Simon said very little while they walked. He kept his eyes firmly on Kannon and watched as the hunched creature pushed through the low branches.

As they neared the fire Kannon craned his neck back. 'You must remember,' he growled. 'What happens tonight must stay within the Circle. You cannot discuss anything that you see or hear with anybody else. Not an adult, nor anyone your own age. It would be devastating to us if our secret came out.'

Simon nodded. 'What happens when we get there?'

'There's no routine,' said Kannon. 'We just talk and

have fun. Whatever you want to do. Some of them like to tell stories and others play games.'

'Do I have to do anything?' said Simon.

'What do you mean?'

'I mean, do I have to do something to become a member of the Secret Circle?'

'You've seen us, so you're a member. All you have to do to remain a member is remember what I've told you.'

Simon and Kannon entered the clearing, and they were instantly hit by the heat of the fire. The surrounding woodland was lit in a yellow and orange glow and the ground had been cleared of the fallen autumn leaves. There was one huge oak tree on the other side of the clearing, its branches sprouting like arms up into the darkness.

There were a dozen green-skinned creatures dotted through the clearing. There were tall ones, short ones, fat ones and skinny ones. Each of them had large heads with big, round eyes.

Along with the creatures were children, some who Simon recognised and others he didn't. Simon could see Amie giggling beside a stocky creature who was flailing his arms in the air.

'Simon!' yelled Jonathon from across the clearing. 'They've finally invited you!'

'Yeah,' said Simon, rather sheepishly.

Jonathon grabbed the arm of one of the creatures and they rounded the bonfire.

'This is Hemlin,' said Jonathon with a nod toward the tall, gangly creature. 'He's my imaginary friend. He can do things with a football you wouldn't believe!'

'Really?' said Simon, forcing a smile.

'Show him, Hemlin!'

Hemlin scurried over to the other side of the clearing and took out a football which had been hidden behind a tree stump. He booted the ball skyward and it disappeared into the star-covered sky.

Jonathon looked at Hemlin expectantly. 'Where did it go?'

Hemlin smiled smugly and held out the palm of his hand so that his long, skinny fingers formed a bowl shape. A short moment later the ball landed perfectly in his hand.

'WOW!' screamed Jonathon. 'That was brilliant!'

'I saw that, that was amazing!' said a dark-skinned boy who hopped out from the woods. Simon recognised him from school.

'Thanks, Jake, I've been practising,' said Hemlin.

'Do it again, Hemlin!'

Hemlin booted the ball again, this time even harder, and it must have been in the air for almost half a minute before it landed perfectly between the creature's outstretched fingers.

'You should play for Chelsea!' said Jake.

'Manchester United, more like!' said Jonathon.

'Or Liverpool!' said Ryan. He had appeared from between two tree trunks and was closely followed by another tall, thin imaginary friend. He waved excitedly as he spotted Simon.

Simon saw others he knew from either school or Hedgely. There was Becky Walker and Lindsey Evans from school, who both gave Simon a wave as they skipped around the circle with their imaginary friends. Simon also spotted Will. He was watching a broad-shouldered creature balance a pile of stones on his forehead like a sea lion.

Simon was introduced to two people he'd never met before: a young boy called Warren Oliver, who was apparently in a lower year at Simon's school, sat staring at the crackling fire; and a girl called Claire Ruttle, who was talking excitedly with Amie and her imaginary friend, known as Grork. The creature had a deep, rasping voice as he told what seemed to be a very exciting story.

A fat creature, introduced to Simon as Rane, clapped his chunky hands loudly together. 'Everybody, if you haven't already met him, this is Simon.'

Simon looked through the crowd and shifted his feet awkwardly as he realised all eyes were on him.

'He is now the tenth member of the Secret Circle,' said Rane. 'All of the same rules apply. If you are anywhere outside of the Circle, then you must not talk to each other about us. You can never be sure where the nearest ears are listening from. Other than that, have fun. Make Simon feel at home!'

Simon relaxed as everyone went back to their previous activities. Children and creatures were scurrying round the fire, and others were throwing a ball back and forth while Ryan and Will played a game of cards. The imaginary friends all had wide grins on their faces and were obviously thrilled to be impressing their audience. Simon was just taking in the sights of everything that was going on around him and hadn't realised that Jake had sat on a tree stump beside him.

'I know you from school, don't I?' he said.

Simon looked at Jake and nodded.

'What do you think of it?' said Jake.

Simon shrugged. 'I don't know,' he said honestly.

'Don't you think it's amazing?'

'It is amazing,' said Simon. 'But it all seems strange to me.'

Jake looked around to make sure nobody was close by. A crowd had gathered around Hemlin, who was demonstrating his football trick again.

'What do you mean?'

'Well, why are they here?' said Simon. 'Where did they come from?'

'They're here to entertain us!' said Jake. 'I don't know where they came from. They say they're our imaginary friends, so… they're from our imaginations, I guess.'

'I've never imagined anything like this before,' said Simon. 'Have you?'

'Not that I know of, but it might have been any one of us who imagined them.'

Simon thought for a second. 'If they're from somebody's imagination, then how come we can all see them?'

'I don't know that either,' said Jake. 'Magic, probably.'

'Do you believe in magic?'

'Not until recently. How else can you explain all this?'

Simon shook his head.

'Everything okay over here?' said Kannon, suddenly appearing over Simon's shoulder.

'Fine, Kannon!' said Jake. He shot to his feet and ran over to join Ryan and Will.

'How about you, Simon?' Kannon sat down on the stump and crossed his thin legs.

'Fine,' said Simon.

'I overheard what you were saying. You are a curious one, aren't you?'

Simon smiled. 'I guess. It's just not every day you meet a real imaginary friend, is it?'

'Very true,' said Kannon with a smile. 'But, you know, if you're not sure you want to be here, you don't have to be. Nobody's forcing you.'

'I know; it's not that I don't want to be here,' said Simon. 'I'm just trying to understand it.'

'There's nothing you need to understand. There aren't any catches with the Secret Circle. You're just here to have fun. Isn't that what all imaginary friends are for?'

'I've never had one before,' said Simon. 'But yeah, I suppose that's why you would have an imaginary friend.'

Kannon nodded. 'Absolutely. You can see us, you can hear us.' He grabbed Simon's wrist and tapped his hand against his bony arm. 'And you can touch us. That's all you need to understand.'

Simon nodded, but only half in agreement.

'You're still unsure?'

'But if we can do all of those things, how can you be imaginary?'

'I don't have all the answers you want, Simon. Just look around — look at everybody here. Do they look like they're worried about the hows and the whys?'

Simon shook his head. Hemlin was flicking the football between his gangly legs while the crowd watched in amazement.

'If it's not what you want then you're free to go home. We're only here to have fun, so switch off your mind for a while and relax.' Kannon winked and patted Simon on the back before joining the others to watch Hemlin's football tricks.

Maybe Kannon was right. Simon was letting the detective within him do all the thinking. He could see how much fun the others were having and how carefree they all seemed around the imaginary friends, so he decided he would let himself go with the flow and try to enjoy it.

CHAPTER NINE

It was almost six o'clock when Simon got back into bed. It felt as if the moment his head hit the soft pillow his alarm announced it was time to get up.

On the way to school, in the back of the car, Simon had a quick nap. His whole body felt limp and he struggled even to walk through the school gates and find his way to the classroom. As he sat down Mrs Ramsworth glared at him over her glasses.

Jonathon, who was slouched down beside Simon, nodded his greeting.

'Last night was so weird,' said Simon.

'Shh,' said Jonathon.

Simon looked at the clock. It wasn't nine o'clock just yet, so they were still allowed to talk.

'I saw some of Hemlin's tricks, they were –'

'Shh!' interrupted Jonathon, this time with a harsher

tone.

'What?'

'Don't you remember the rules?'

'Yeah,' said Simon. 'But nobody can hear.'

'It doesn't matter,' said Jonathon. 'You don't know that.'

'You didn't even give me a chance to say anything!'

'Exactly. They'll get mad if you do.'

'But you're talking about them now.'

Jonathon growled. 'Just don't say anything. You'll get kicked out if you do, so just do what they say.'

The bell rang and Mrs Ramsworth opened her register. 'Samantha?'

'Here.'

'How long have you been in the Secret Circle, anyway?' Simon whispered.

Jonathon didn't respond.

'Hey? How long?'

'Mr Andrews!' snapped Mrs Ramsworth. 'Be quiet!'

Simon ducked his head.

'Yeah,' said Jonathon. 'Be quiet.'

***

'Mr Andrews!'

Simon felt himself awaken with a jolt, and his stomach performed a somersault.

'Yes?' he said groggily.

'You have decided that you want to join your fellow students in detention for sleeping in my class, I see? Get to the headmaster's office.'

'But –'

'Now.'

***

Mr Cricklewood gave Simon a long, minty-fresh lecture on the importance of paying attention in class. He had been joined by the boy Warren from Year Four who Simon had seen at the Secret Circle. Warren had fallen asleep in Maths, and it had been the third time in a week he had been sent to the headmaster's office.

After their lecture, Simon and Warren had been made to sit outside Mr Cricklewood's office while he wrote angry letters to their parents.

'I'm not surprised you've done this three times,' said Simon, making sure to keep his voice down. 'I don't think I've ever been this tired.'

Warren kept his eyes fixed on a spot on the worn, grey carpet and swung his legs anxiously beneath the chair.

'Yeah,' he said.

'How long have you been in the Secret Circle?'

Warren didn't look away from the ground but he winced like something hurt.

'How long?'

'We can't talk about this here,' said Warren. 'You need to keep it inside the Circle.'

'There's nobody around; everybody's in lessons.'

Warren shook his head. 'No. I can't.'

Simon slouched down in his chair and rolled his eyes. He found it very frustrating that nobody was willing to bend the rules even a little.

'Look, I'll show you,' said Simon. He looked up and down the narrow corridor and shouted 'Hello?'

There was no reply.

'See,' he said.

Warren shrugged. 'They're magic. You don't know what powers they have.'

'They can do football tricks and make funny noises, they don't have supersonic hearing,' said Simon.

'You don't know what they can do,' said Warren. 'They're imaginary. They can do whatever you imagine them to do.'

'So if I made a picture in my head of a giant pink elephant dancing in a pool of strawberry jelly with Kannon singing the Macarena, are you telling me it would happen?'

Warren scratched his head. 'Maybe.'

Simon laughed. In a strange way, he hoped it would. He'd have loved to have seen something like that.

'Boys! In here!' bellowed Mr Cricklewood.

Simon and Warren scurried into the headmaster's office for another round of lectures.

***

That night Simon only managed to stay awake until half past seven. He played video games with his dad, who had returned from his trip, but halfway through a game of football he closed his eyes. When he woke up he was losing 7-0.

'I need to go to bed,' said Simon.

'Try and sleep through the night, tonight.'

'I know,' said Simon, and he trudged off to bed without even brushing his teeth.

CHAPTER TEN

'Wake up,' said Kannon.

Simon felt himself awaken but he didn't open his eyes.

'Hey, Simon,' repeated the creature. 'We're meeting at the Secret Circle tonight.'

Simon shook his head. He wanted to do nothing other than sleep.

'Come on, we can't be late. Wake up.'

Simon opened his eyes and saw the bony frame of Kannon crouching over him. The clock on the bedside table was blinking quarter to three.

'Not tonight,' said Simon.

'But you're a member now,' said Kannon. 'You can't miss a meeting.'

'Why?'

'There are so many things to do! I think Hemlin has

been practising a new trick with Thump!'

'I'll see it another night.' Simon closed his eyes and pulled the bedcovers over his chin.

Kannon leant in a little closer. 'You have to come,' he said. 'I'm your imaginary friend now, so you have to come with me to the Secret Circle.'

'Tired.' Simon said. He was barely awake enough to speak.

'Okay, it's your choice,' said Kannon. 'But don't expect to be invited back again.'

Simon opened his eyes. 'Why?'

'Once you're in the Secret Circle, you are committed to your imaginary friend,' said Kannon. He had pulled the door open slightly and was halfway out of the room.

'But why?'

'I don't make the rules, Simon.'

Simon sat up and rubbed his eyes. 'Who does?'

Kannon huffed and moved his whole body back into the room. 'You ask too many questions. Maybe I was too hasty in my decision in inviting you into the Secret Circle. I thought you were going to be more like your sister. She's already on her way. She's not worried about sleep, or why we have to do what we do.'

'Amie's already gone?' said Simon.

'About ten minutes ago. She'll be in the woods by

now.'

Simon couldn't find a reason to argue about going any more. His sister was out in the woods somewhere, so the big brother inside him forced him out of bed, and he crept downstairs to slip on his trainers.

CHAPTER ELEVEN

Kannon had a wide grin spread across his large featured face. It was a cool night and Simon was glad he had remembered to take his coat before they headed out. The star-littered sky had scatterings of grey cloud, and the wind was kicking up waves of crunchy autumn leaves.

Simon was greeted by everyone like he had been a member of the Secret Circle for years. Even the imaginary friends who Simon hadn't spoken to before were enthusiastic with their welcome. Simon spotted Warren talking to the stocky creature known as Rane, and Amie was laughing and talking with Grork.

Kannon and Simon had not been the last to arrive at the Secret Circle. Ryan and his imaginary friend Randall arrived just in time to watch Hemlin rebound a football between two trees.

'He's good, isn't he?' Ryan said to Simon. 'I wish

Liverpool had players as good as him.'

'I don't think you're allowed to have imaginary friends play for your team,' said Simon.

'That's true, but if nobody saw them then imagine how many goals they'd score! We'd beat everybody!'

'How are you doing, boys?' said a short, squashed-faced creature Simon hadn't spoken to before.

'Fine,' said Ryan.

'Good,' said the creature. He turned to Simon and smiled. 'I don't believe we've been introduced. I'm Zam. I'm Claire's imaginary friend.'

Simon shook the creature's outstretched hand. His fingers were long and thin and they wrapped around Simon's hand like a claw game from a seaside arcade.

'So what were you two talking about?'

'Football,' said Ryan. 'I was saying I wish Hemlin played for Liverpool!'

Zam nodded but Simon knew he didn't have a clue who Liverpool were.

'So you like football as well, Simon?'

Simon nodded.

'Do you have a favourite team?'

Simon shook his head. 'Not really. I like Manchester United, but don't really support anyone like Ryan does.'

'Does your dad like football?' asked Zam.

Simon paused for a second. 'Yeah, he loves it.'

'Does he have a favourite team?'

'Manchester United. That's why I sort of like them.'

'Has he ever been to see them play?'

'When he was younger, I think.'

'Why not now?'

Simon shrugged. 'We live too far away. He lived closer to Manchester when he was my age.'

'Why did he move?'

'He got a job here after he met my Mum.'

'Where does he work?'

'For a bank. Why?'

'I'm just trying to get to know you better,' said Zam.

'It's okay, Simon,' said Ryan. 'Zam always asks about our parents.'

'It's just a little habit of mine,' said Zam. 'I can tell you Lindsay's dad is a farmer, Jake's dad is a shop manager, and Warren's dad is a salesman. Did you know Amie's dad works in a bank as well?'

Ryan chuckled and Zam's expression darkened.

'What?' he growled.

'Amie's my sister,' said Simon.

'Oh, really?' said Zam. His top lip flicked slightly on each side baring his needle-sharp teeth for a brief moment. 'Excuse me for a second.'

Simon watched as Zam crossed the clearing and stood with Rane, who was watching the bonfire cast bright orange flecks into the sky. After exchanging a few words they both walked away and disappeared into the surrounding woods.

'Wonder what they're talking about,' said Simon but, as he turned to look at Ryan, he noticed he'd gone to talk to another imaginary friend who was playing cards with Jake.

'Hi, Simon.'

Amie had appeared in front of him. She was holding her teddy bear tightly and was looking down at her brother, who now sat on a stump.

'You okay?'

Amie nodded. She shook slightly and her nod lasted a little longer than she'd meant it to.

'You look cold.'

'I am a little.'

'Why didn't you bring your coat?'

'Grork said there wasn't enough time.'

'Did he?' Simon looked over the crowd of children and imaginary friends. Grork was sitting at the other side of the fire, speaking to Lindsay and Claire. They were huddled closely together, looking scared and excited at the creature's story.

Simon stood up and his sister had to crane her neck

up to look at him.

'Here,' he said. Simon slipped off his jacket and draped it over his sister's shoulders. 'Wait here a second.'

Simon crossed the clearing and approached Grork and the girls. As he neared, he could hear the creature's story.

'…and then I walked up to the beast and stole the box from him! I was quick, so the monster didn't hear, but when he noticed it was missing he was mad! I…' Grork trailed off as he noticed Simon staring. 'Yes?'

Simon hadn't expected to get this far. His legs had taken him to Grork, but his brain certainly hadn't given them the instruction to do so. Simon had *imagined* himself marching over to Grork and giving him a stern piece of his mind, but never did he think he would actually *do* it. But there he was, standing by the bulky green creature, his eyes fixed on him while he fumbled for some words.

'Can I have a word?' Simon spluttered.

Grork nodded and excused himself from the girls. He then took Simon to a space beside the fire where there were no nearby ears, and invited Simon to speak. With Grork now standing, Simon was completely covered by the creature's shadow.

'Umm, I just wondered why you didn't let Amie take her coat.'

Grork looked at Simon, a confused look in his glassy eyes. A moment later he grinned widely. 'We were in a rush. Didn't want to be late.'

'Amie's cold, she's shivering. She's only seven years old. She needs to wear her coat if she's going out on a night like this.'

Grork nodded and he let his smile fade.

'I can see that you care about your sister,' he said. 'And you're new to the Circle, so I'll let this pass. But don't throw around accusations unless you're certain about something. It can do far more harm than good. Handbag?'

Simon paused. 'What?'

'Okay?'

'What did you say just now?'

'Nothing. Excuse me; I need to finish my story.'

Grork returned to the tree stump beside Lindsay and Claire, the earth shuddering with each heavy step. The creature sat down and continued talking like nothing had happened.

CHAPTER TWELVE

Simon got back into bed at half past five that morning. He had snuck in with Amie and put his trainers back on the shoe rack beside the front door. He hung his coat on the hook, making sure to leave everything how it had been before he left, and he and his sister made their way upstairs. Simon managed two hours of sleep before he was awakened by his alarm clock. He showered and dressed and headed downstairs to get some breakfast before school.

'Good morning,' said Brian, who was sitting at the kitchen table.

'Morning, Dad,' said Simon. 'How are you?'

'Fine,' he said. 'Sleep okay?'

Simon nodded. 'Okay. Better than yesterday.'

'Probably because of the early night, eh?'

Simon stopped pouring his cereal and looked at his dad, whose face was stony. Brian was usually cranky in the morning, but this morning he seemed even crankier than usual. His annoyance seemed to be fuelled by a scratching sound which came from the hallway.

'What's that?'

'Perhaps you can tell me.'

Simon crossed the kitchen and stood in the doorway to the hall. His mum was down on her knees, her work blouse speckled with dirt. She was scrubbing furiously at the carpet, which had a trail of muddy footprints leading from the front door and into the living room.

Simon spun back to face his dad. 'It wasn't me.'

'Who was it, then? Gremlins?'

Simon bit his tongue.

***

Simon was late for school that morning. He had been made to scrub the carpet with his mum, and they didn't leave until all the mud was gone. While he cleaned, Simon thought back to the night before. He was sure he had wiped his feet on the doormat before he put his trainers on the shoe rack. He wasn't just sure, he was positive. He hadn't walked through any mud on the way back from the Secret Circle and there hadn't been mud on his trainers when he put them back on the rack.

But there they were in the rack, caked in thick, sticky mud.

No matter what Simon said, his parents weren't interested in listening. He didn't want to lie, but the truth would have sounded crazy. He and his sister went into the woods to sit around a campfire while a green creature played football? Even to Simon it sounded crazy, so he tried to convince them he'd been sleepwalking.

'Just because your sister can get away with that excuse doesn't mean you can,' said Helen, when she eventually drove them to school. 'And now your sister is late for school as well, so I hope you're happy.'

'It's true,' Simon grumbled.

They drove the rest of the way to school in silence, which was a nice thought to remember when Simon finally opened the door to Mrs Ramsworth's class. She had already finished the morning register by the time he tried to sneak into the room, but as she drew a graph on the whiteboard she hissed like a preying snake.

'You're becoming quite the little rebel, Mr Andrews. You'll be able to find your way to Mr Cricklewood's office in the dark before too long.'

***

According to the school secretary, Mr Cricklewood had to go home because his wife had called him, worrying she'd left the gas on at home, so he wouldn't be back in until later that afternoon. Simon was sent to an empty classroom where he was made to write lines until the end of the mid-morning break.

At eleven o'clock the door opened and Jonathon Turner walked sheepishly into the classroom. Simon watched as he sat down and rested his head into his folded arms.

'What did you do?' said Simon.

Jonathon sighed. 'What do you think?'

'What time did you get home last night?'

Jonathon didn't answer.

'Hey?'

Jonathon raised his head. 'Shush.'

'No, come on, tell me. I got in at half past five.'

Jonathon dug his head back into his crossed arms.

'Six,' he mumbled.

'You were late, what were you doing?'

Jonathon groaned.

'Were you watching Hemlin?'

Jonathon's head shot up. 'Shh! Don't say their names.'

'Why?'

'Because. It's the rules.'

'They can't hear. It's not like they have cameras round the school watching and listening to everything that goes on.'

'They might.'

Jonathon sank back into his chair and closed his eyes.

'Tired?' Simon asked with a smile.

'I feel like I haven't slept in a month.'

'A month? Is that how long you've been going to the Secret Circle?'

Jonathon twitched but didn't answer.

'Is it?'

He nodded.

'What about everybody else?'

Jonathon shrugged.

'Jonathon?'

'About the same, I think. Some a lot less, like you. Quiet now, you don't know who might be listening.'

'Like who, the secretary? Is Thump here? Maybe he's hiding behind the whiteboard?'

'Shh!'

'Or is Rane hiding in the bin, perhaps? He's pretty big so it might be a tight squeeze.'

'Simon, do you want to get us both punished? Don't talk about them. They know when you do. I don't know how, but they do.'

Simon frowned. 'Punished?'

'If you break the rules, you'll be punished. Or worse, they'll kick you out of the Secret Circle.'

'Punished how?'

'I don't know. There was this kid from a few villages over from Hedgely. His name was Luke. He told his brother about it, I think…'

'And?'

'He didn't come back. He was sent to live with his uncle.'

'Why?'

'Something happened, but I don't know what. Must have been serious if his parents sent him away.'

Simon felt his stomach turn and thought back to earlier that morning.

'Would they do something like… walk mud through your house?'

'Well, that's not serious enough to send you away… why? Did they…?'

'There was mud on my trainers this morning, and footprints all over the carpet. I know I didn't do it when I got home last night.'

Jonathon shifted uncomfortably. 'What have you done?'

'Nothing,' said Simon.

'You must have done something,' said Jonathon. His eyes were wide and unblinking.

'I haven't, honest,' said Simon.

'Well it sounds like you've annoyed somebody.'

CHAPTER THIRTEEN

That night, Simon and Amie were taken out for a meal with their parents. It wasn't to celebrate anything in particular, but Helen had been short-tempered while she drove them home, and flopped in the armchair as soon as they got back.

'I can't be bothered to cook tonight,' she said.

'What's wrong?' said Amie. She had turned on the television and was watching a dog chase a cat around a supermarket.

'Work.'

'What about work?'

'Nothing seemed to go right today. There was our little incident this morning, which was a nice start. When I got to work my boss sent me some important files to make copies of, but they've gone walkabouts somewhere. And to make things worse, my computer decided to block me from using it, so I spent all afternoon trying to get that sorted.'

'Oh,' said Amie, but she hadn't taken her eyes away from the TV.

Simon tried to sneak the remote control away from his sister, but she spotted him and nudged it out of reach.

After Simon had been enduring his sister's favourite show for about an hour, Brian arrived home and they all headed out to the restaurant, which was a few villages over from Hedgely. Simon tried to keep himself as unnoticed as possible, as the muddy carpet certainly hadn't been forgotten.

'No video games for a week,' his dad had said.

Simon managed to fight the urge to argue.

'And no pudding tonight.'

'Can I have pudding?' said Amie.

'If you like.'

Amie smiled and poked her tongue at her brother while their parents browsed the menu. Simon had given up on his sleepwalking story and had decided the easiest thing to do was take the punishment. He didn't want to be sent to the funny farm for trying to convince them that he thought his imaginary friend did it.

The restaurant was loud and busy. It was their favourite place to go, as it had so many different kinds of food, and Simon never had any difficulty choosing. He ordered pizza, the same as his sister, while their parents ordered pasta and shared a bottle of wine. Once their food arrived, Simon was glad that the conversation moved away from that morning's incident.

'I looked all over for those files,' Helen said. 'I've no idea where they went, and everybody swears blind that they didn't touch them.'

'I know the feeling,' said Brian. 'Similar thing happened to me yesterday. Found a major client's file tucked between the radiator and the wall after it went missing. No idea what happened there.'

Simon ate in silence and listened to his parents. He felt one of them knock his leg beneath the table, but neither of them owned up or apologised for it and they just carried on moaning about work.

Simon felt another knock beneath the table, this time on the leg nearest his sister. He winced but said nothing and gave his sister an angry glare.

'Mum, tell Simon to stop pulling faces at me.'

'Stop it, Simon,' said Helen before returning to her conversation.

Simon didn't argue.

There was another kick, this time harder, and Simon had to bite his tongue to stop him from yelling.

Stop it, he mouthed without saying the words.

'What?' his sister whispered.

'You know what.'

Simon was kicked again, this time a lot harder. His knee smacked hard in to the underside of the table and knocked Brian's glass of wine all over his plate of pasta.

***

Even the restaurant offering Brian a fresh plate of pasta couldn't stop Simon from being punished again. Not only was he banned from playing video games for three weeks, he was grounded for two weeks as well.

They arrived home at eight o'clock and Simon was marched to his room, despite his attempts to convince them his sister was kicking him beneath the table. Simon didn't care that his sister's legs didn't even reach the floor; he had felt the kicks and could already see the bruises on his knees.

At half past eight Simon heard Amie being put to bed, and at eleven o'clock his parents switched off all the lights and the door to their bedroom clicked shut. His mind was far too switched on to think about sleep. He had been sprawled on top of his covers with his eyes fixed on the ceiling while a flurry of things whizzed through his mind.

He had a lot to ask Kannon about.

At midnight, Simon watched the clock. Each minute seemed to last twice as long and, at one point, Simon was sure time went backwards.

He rubbed his eyes. All this lack of sleep must have been playing tricks on him.

At quarter past one there was a creak out in the hallway. Simon shot up into a sitting position and listened. He held his breath and stared at the door, but the sound didn't happen again.

At half past one there was a groan from somewhere deeper in the house. It didn't sound like a footstep, and the house was so old it would shift and shuffle all the time regardless of whether or not somebody was moving around.

Simon must have fallen asleep, because the next time he looked at the clock it had just passed four o'clock in the morning. The door was shut and he was alone in the room.

Kannon had obviously not been.

Simon sat up and stretched. Through his window he could see it was a calm, cloudless night. Even the night-time wildlife was silent.

Perhaps there wasn't a meeting? Maybe Tuesday was a day off for the Secret Circle?

Kannon hadn't mentioned anything like that. He hadn't said there wouldn't be a meeting that night.

Simon slipped out of bed and pulled open his bedroom door. The hallway was dark, but Simon could see just enough to avoid the noisy floorboards and move over to his sister's bedroom door, which was slightly ajar. As he slid into the room he could just make out the empty space in Amie's bed.

Simon grunted and moved as fast as he could while still remaining silent. He hopped between the safe floorboards of the hallway and almost slipped as he scurried down the stairs. At the front door he jumped into his trainers, which had taken him twenty minutes to clean that morning, and snatched his coat from the rail. It was a cold night outside, and it was obvious that the Secret Circle was meeting without him.

CHAPTER FOURTEEN

Simon ducked between the shadows as he made his way between houses and cars in the direction of the woods. The only sound for miles around was the trickle of the stream which ran through the village green. Even the scattered clumps of autumn leaves lay undisturbed.

Simon climbed the bank on the outskirts of the woodland and was shrouded in darkness as he entered the trees. The moonlight struggled to squeeze between the tangled branches above, so Simon moved forward with his arms outstretched to stop himself from knocking into trees.

Usually Simon would be able to see the distant glow of the fire in the centre of the Secret Circle, but no matter how much he squinted, he just couldn't see anything ahead.

Simon tripped on a buried root and his shoulder cracked hard into a thick tree trunk. His whole upper arm throbbed, but he picked himself up, brushed the crushed bark from his coat, and moved on.

Where was the fire? It was hard to judge the distance in the dark, but Simon was sure he wasn't far away. He couldn't hear anything but the crunch of leaves beneath his feet.

He wanted to call out, he wanted to scream so they knew he was coming, but if the fire wasn't burning, would there be anybody there to hear?

What if they had changed the meeting place? Did they meet somewhere else on Tuesday nights? Simon's stomach knotted at the thought of Kannon turning up in his bedroom to see he'd gone. Would Kannon and the other imaginary friends even care that he wasn't there? Would they go looking for him?

Simon pushed on. He'd give it a couple more minutes and then turn back.

An owl hooted. It was the first sign of life Simon had come across, and it was a welcome break from the uncomfortable silence.

Just ahead, Simon spotted a clearing. His walk turned into a jog and, after another brief stumble, he broke out into the clearing. It was definitely the Secret Circle; Simon could make out the space in the centre where the fire usually was. Around it were the tree stumps arranged neatly, but they were all empty. It didn't look like anybody had been there for a while.

'Amie?' he said. 'Kannon? Anyone?'

Silence.

Simon circled the fire, but saw nothing to suggest that anyone had been there. If there was a meeting tonight, Simon was either in the wrong place or it hadn't started yet.

Simon glanced at the cloudless sky above. Perhaps the meeting was starting late? Simon let himself fall back onto a tree stump. It wouldn't be too much longer till the sun started to rise, so surely it wouldn't start now.

'Hello?' he yelled, but he didn't expect a response.

He gave up after that. Simon trudged back through the woodland, kicking up leaves like miniature explosions. As he reached the edge of the trees and saw the houses at the bottom of the bank, Simon had to shield his eyes from a bright light. He felt the urge to turn and run back into the woods, but a familiar voice, in a furious, screeching tone, made him come out from the trees.

'Simon Andrews, come down here at once!' screamed Helen.

Chapter Fifteen

Helen drove Simon home and ordered him to bed. Simon had never seen her quite so red-faced — that was, until he told her that he was going to find Amie, who hadn't been in her bed.

'She'd been to the toilet!' she growled.

'But —'

'I don't want to hear it!'

Simon kept quiet for the rest of the short trip home. Once he was back in bed his dad marched into the room. He was getting used to these lectures now and, if he was honest with himself, he could understand why his parents were giving them to him. When he thought about it, what he was part of was crazy. He and his friends were sneaking out at night, while their parents slept, to meet a bunch of green creatures that played cards and did tricks.

It was crazy. So why couldn't Simon stop thinking

about it?

When his dad finally left to go back to bed, Simon didn't think about going to sleep. The questions he had for the imaginary friends were only increasing in number, his trip to the woods had answered nothing and, instead, his mind was spinning. No matter what reason he came up with, he just could not make sense of it.

Why was there no meeting?

Why had Kannon not visited?

Had Amie really just been in the toilet when he looked into her room?

Were the footprints something to do with the imaginary friends?

The questions jumbled into a ball and Simon was beginning to confuse himself.

Somewhere in the darkness the house groaned.

'Kannon?' he said.

There was no reply.

***

The next morning things didn't get much better for Simon. After washing and getting dressed he went downstairs and was greeted by his parents, who were sat at the kitchen table reading a letter. Simon recognised the logo on the letter and his heart beat just that little bit faster.

'You fell asleep in a lesson?' said Brian. 'Simon, this is getting silly now.'

'I know,' Simon said.

'What do we have to do to get through to you? Sneaking out at night, traipsing mud in onto the carpet, falling asleep at school. This has all got to stop.'

Simon nodded. He was desperate to tell his parents everything. They thought he was going mad, and he wanted to set the whole thing straight. But the truth was far madder than anything he could make up.

'I have to go to London again for a couple of nights,' said Brian. 'And when I get back I want to hear from your mother that everything is back to normal. I want to know that you've stayed in your room all night, you've been awake through school, and everything else is back to being how it was. I just don't know what's wrong with you at the moment.'

'Nothing's wrong,' muttered Simon.

'Well, something isn't right.'

***

Simon was desperate to stay awake during morning lessons. He managed to get through geography without any problems, but a boring lecture during science had his head dipping dangerously close to his desk.

As soon as the bell rang Simon packed away his things and was the first to burst out of the doors and into the playground. The air was cool and fresh, and it helped to wake him up just a little bit.

Abdul and David were out soon after and spotted Simon sitting on a bench by the mobile classroom.

'Simon!' yelled Abdul. 'Come and have a game of football with us.'

'No thanks.'

'Come on, we need a goalkeeper.'

'Ask somebody else.'

'No, you're better in goal, come on.'

'I'm too tired to play.'

'You too? What is wrong with you lot? I think you all need to go to bed a bit earlier.'

Abdul and David disappeared behind the assembly hall and the sound of the ball bouncing on the gravel echoed between the old stone walls of the school.

The playground soon filled up. The younger ones from the years below Simon were darting around and playing while older groups stood in circles gossiping and laughing.

Simon could see Jonathon and Jake leaning against the wall talking quietly to each other, so he made his way across the playground to join them.

Whatever they had been talking about, they stopped as they saw Simon approach.

'I need to ask you something,' Simon said.

'Depends what it is,' said Jake.

'What do you mean?'

Jonathon and Jake exchanged glances.

'What do you want to ask us about?' said Jonathon.

Simon looked over his shoulder to make sure there was nobody nearby.

'Kannon didn't show up last night.'

'Shut up!' said Jake a little too loudly, which drew some strange looks from others in the playground.

'I just need to know something,' said Simon in a gruff whisper.

'Shh,' said Jonathon.

'Was there a meeting last night?'

'Shush!'

'Just say yes or no.'

'Yes or no.'

Simon sighed. 'Jake, was there?'

Jake thought for a moment.

'Well?'

'No,' he said finally. 'Now shh.'

'What were you guys talking about before I came

over? You seemed pretty keen to talk then.'

'Nothing,' Jonathon said.

'Didn't look like it to me. Come on, nobody's listening.'

'You don't know that.'

'I do,' said Simon. He outstretched his hands and spun on the spot. 'See, nobody here.' He moved away from Jonathon and Jake and kept spinning, stretching his arms out further. 'Look, see!'

Simon nudged into something and his arms instantly shot down to his sides. He turned to apologise to whoever he'd knocked into, but he was nowhere near anybody else in the playground. He was, however, being watched by a group of girls and, when he looked back at them, they giggled. Simon quickly rejoined Jonathon and Jake by the wall and didn't look back.

'So, come on, what were you talking about?' said Simon.

Jake frowned. 'You,' he snapped.

'What do you mean?'

'Jon told me about what happened. The footprints.'

'So?'

'So you need to stop doing whatever it is you're doing.'

'Last night was the first night in ages where there

hasn't been a meeting,' added Jonathon. 'I was looking forward to it, as well.'

'You think that's because of me?' said Simon.

'It must be. You're breaking the rules, so do us a favour and stop it before you get us all into trouble.'

'Or even better, just stop going to the Secret Circle altogether,' said Jake.

'Shh,' said Jonathon. He gave Jake a wide-eyed, worried look.

Jake took a deep breath. 'Just go,' he said.

So Simon left.

CHAPTER SIXTEEN

For the rest of the day Simon kept to himself. At lunch he sat in the library and searched for books about imaginary friends, but the closest thing he found was a children's book about a boy who had an invisible pet monkey who liked to cause mischief.

Well, the mischief part was certainly the same.

Gossip had clearly spread around the other members of the Secret Circle, as they did their best to avoid Simon. Warren had even gone as far as completely turning around and walking away when they approached one another in the corridor.

What Simon had done to upset everyone, he had no idea, but it was just another question to add to his ever-growing list.

That night they arrived home and Simon was desperate to speak to Amie on her own for a moment. He had yet to find even a minute to ask her about the Secret Circle and, after dinner, as the two of them sat watching television with their mum, it looked unlikely that he would get a chance to speak to her again.

'Bedtime, kids,' said Helen at half past eight.

Without a word, Amie headed upstairs.

'It's early,' said Simon.

'I don't think you have any cause to argue,' she said. 'I want you to go to bed and not leave that room until morning.'

'What if I need the toilet?'

'Then cross your legs. Take a bucket into your room. I don't care. Just stay in that room until I tell you to come out. I don't think I can take another night of chasing you around the village.'

Simon could think of nothing to say to that, so he too headed upstairs and got ready for bed.

***

It didn't taken Simon long to fall asleep, and it didn't take him long to wake up shortly after that. He could hear Amie talking through the wall, and her voice switched on his brain like a bulb.

'Hello?' he whispered.

There was no reply.

'Hello? Kannon?'

There was still no answer. Amie chatted away, but Simon couldn't hear anybody talking back. Maybe Grork had a surprisingly quiet whisper on him despite his massive size.

'Amie?' he grunted, trying not to be too loud.

The room next door fell silent.

'Amie?'

Nothing.

'I know you can hear me,' he said. 'I can hear you in there, so I know you can hear me.'

Still silence.

'Is Grork in there with you? Can you ask him if Kannon is coming tonight?'

After a moment Amie whispered again as if Simon hadn't even spoken.

Simon groaned. It was only midnight, still early, so maybe Kannon would come in the next few hours?

At two o'clock, Kannon still hadn't shown himself. Amie still chatted happily and Simon struggled to stay awake. At half past two there was a groan somewhere in the hallway. Simon snorted himself awake, but it wasn't interesting enough to even raise his head from the pillow.

That was, until Simon heard a laugh somewhere outside.

He shot out of bed and over to the window. He peered out through a small crack in the curtains and looked over towards the village green. The sky was layered with cloud except for a small slit which let streams of moonlight streak across the nearby houses.

It was just enough light for Simon to see his sister walk hand in hand with Grork across the grass and over toward the woodland.

Simon spun on the spot. 'Kannon?' he said. 'Are you in here?'

He didn't expect an answer, and he didn't get one.

Outside, Amie and Grork were almost out of view. If it hadn't been for a lamppost on the other side of the village green Simon wouldn't have been able to see his sister at all.

He now had a decision to make and hardly any time to make it.

Should he follow and risk getting in even deeper trouble, or should he wake up his mum and risk exposing the Secret Circle?

Neither were choices he wanted to make, but he was desperately searching for a third option.

Should he just go back to bed and ignore it completely? No.

Should he wait for Kannon to appear? No.

Should he open the window and scream into the village? Definitely no.

Simon was already in trouble with his parents – would venturing out into the woods once more really make things much worse? Maybe. Simon hadn't seen his parents that angry in a long time, not since he was ten and kicked his football through the living room window.

He was also in trouble with his friends. They already thought he was spoiling the Secret Circle for them, so exposing the whole thing certainly wouldn't help to make them feel any better.

What was there left to do?

Simon had never done it before, but he'd certainly thought about it a few times. He yanked open his curtains, opened his window as wide as it would go, and pulled himself up onto the windowsill. The way the old-fashioned thatched roof arched down either side and beneath the window meant Simon could easily shimmy down. He clung tightly to the rough straw, which crunched under his weight and, as he reached the lowest point, he leant out and grabbed a sturdy branch of an overhanging apple tree.

His upper arms throbbed, but Simon managed to lower himself down just enough so he could fall a short distance onto the small patch of grass in the front garden.

At least his mum wouldn't hear him sneaking

through the hallway. He could almost picture her with her ear pressed up against her bedroom door listening for the sound of movement.

Simon made his way through the village, his socks already soaked from the damp grass of the green.

CHAPTER SEVENTEEN

It didn't take Simon long to catch up to Amie. She was alone, but her hand was up in the air like it had been the first night he had followed her into the woods.

Where had Grork gone?

There was an icy breeze running through the village and Simon could already feel his toes starting to numb. The dark clouds thickened fast and the strips of moonlight which broke through were starting to disappear.

Simon could see Amie didn't have her coat on. She was out in the freezing night with nothing but her little white nightgown and her stuffed bear.

As Amie reached the bank to the woods, she made her way up the dirt path and met up with Claire Ruttle, who was with an imaginary friend Simon hadn't been introduced to. It had small legs like a dog, but a bulky, broad-shouldered body which was topped off by a tiny round head. It looked like it might topple over at any moment.

Simon watched as Amie, Claire, and the imaginary friend vanished inside the woods.

Simon thought about it for a second. If he went in after them there would be no turning back. It might have even been too late already; his mum could have checked his room that very second. He didn't want to imagine the look on her face or the furious phone calls she would be making.

He looked behind. There was no sign of a car screeching through the village.

Not yet, anyway.

Simon followed his sister into the woods.

***

Simon kept his distance, but could still see Amie, Claire, and the imaginary friend ahead. Amie still had her hand held out like she was holding an umbrella.

It took them ten minutes to reach the Secret Circle. The crackling fire had been their guide; it seemed to be bigger and was burning much brighter. It coated the whole woodland with its warmth.

The clearing was already busy with people and imaginary friends. It looked as though the meeting was well under way without him.

As Amie and Claire entered the clearing they were greeted by cheerful welcomes. The two girls immediately joined in with some sort of game Hemlin was playing with Warren and Jake.

Simon crept closer to the clearing. The warmth from the fire completely made Simon forget that it was a freezing night, and his toes already had the feeling returning to them. The whole group seemed oblivious to Simon's absence. Either that, or they didn't care.

On the other side of the fire something caught his eye and Simon had to move forward another step to see more clearly. He stood on his tiptoes and squinted, just to make sure he was seeing it right.

It was Kannon. He was sitting on a tree stump away from the group talking to somebody. Simon craned his neck further to help make out who it was.

Abdul.

Simon held his chest as his heart began drumming heavily against the inside of his ribs. It took him a moment to realise that, even though the drumming was loud to him, there was no way the others could hear it.

They could, however, hear the crunch of a branch beneath Simon's feet.

Jonathon looked across and his eyes met Simon's.

'Simon?'

Simon held his finger to his lips, but it was too late. Grork and the lopsided imaginary friend had already seen him and were striding over to meet him.

Simon looked back. There was nowhere to run now.

'Hi,' he said as he stepped into the clearing. The games had stopped and all eyes were focused on Simon. He shifted his feet and cleared his throat loudly.

'What are you doing here?' said the strange creature with small legs and fat upper body.

'Come on now, Ralcar, that's no way to greet somebody.' Kannon placed his slender hand on the odd creature's shoulder and the two of them switched places. 'How are you, Simon?'

'I'm okay,' said Simon. 'Just a little confused.'

'We thought you were grounded,' said Jonathon, who was standing in the crowd of onlookers.

'I was,' said Simon. 'I mean, I am.'

'That's why we didn't come to see you tonight,' said Kannon. 'We didn't want to get you into any more trouble, did we?'

A few of the surrounding imaginary friends shook their heads.

'You could have come to tell me,' said Simon.

'That's true, and for that I am sorry,' said the creature. 'We were just thinking of your best interests.'

Simon looked across the clearing and saw Abdul. He smiled nervously and waved.

'What about Abdul?' said Simon. 'Are you his imaginary friend now?'

'No,' said Kannon. 'He has his own.'

'Who?'

Kannon smiled. 'Still full of questions, I see. You would make an excellent defective.'

Simon paused. 'Defective?'

'Detective,' said Ralcar. 'You would make an excellent detective.'

'Indeed,' said Kannon. He clapped his hands together and turned to address the crowd. 'Come on now everyone, it's great news that our friend Simon has joined us, so let's carry on with what we were doing.'

The group parted and everybody returned to playing, talking, and laughing.

'Simon, why don't you speak to Abdul,' said Kannon. 'I believe you know him from school and I'm sure he has lots of questions. The two of you should get along just fine.'

Simon nodded and walked around the fire. It was certainly very hot up close.

'Hi, Simon,' said Abdul. 'I didn't know you were a part of this.'

Simon smiled. 'For a moment there I didn't think I was, either. I only came here for the first time a few days ago.'

'Well, at least it makes sense why a load of you guys were falling asleep in lessons. I'm never going to make it through school tomorrow; it took us about two hours to walk here from my house. Even if I left now I wouldn't get back till about four o'clock. How long do these things last?'

'A few hours,' said Simon. 'You really walked all the way here?'

Abdul nodded. 'Yeah, I know. It's a long way, huh?'

Simon nodded. Abdul lived in a village nearby which took almost fifteen minutes to drive to. He really wouldn't have fancied the walk from there.

'Hello, Simon.' Zam sat on the stump beside Abdul and smiled. He had a large slash down one side of his face which Simon hadn't noticed before. It was bright red and didn't look very old. Dried blood seemed to have stained his thin fingers.

'Hi,' said Simon. 'What happened to your face?'

'Oh, nothing,' said Zam. 'Just an accident. So, you're Abdul? My name is Zam. Pleased to meet you.'

Abdul and Zam shook hands.

'I hear you had a bit of a walk tonight?'

Abdul nodded. 'I come from Clayton, it's quite far.'

'Absolutely,' said Zam with a wide grin. 'Did you manage to get out of your house without being spotted, then?'

'I think so,' he said. 'I don't think my parents noticed at all.'

'That's good. Do you think they would be angry if they found out you were gone?'

'I guess,' said Abdul.

'All of our parents would be, wouldn't they?' said Simon.

Zam ignored Simon. 'What about your dad, would he get really mad?'

'Yeah.'

'What does your dad do for a job?'

'He's a butcher.'

'A butcher?'

'Yeah, he has his own shop in Clayton. I really hope he doesn't notice I'm gone. He tends to get up early to take in the deliveries.'

'Deliveries of what?' said Zam.

Abdul smiled. 'Meat. That's what butchers do. They chop up meat and sell it to people.'

Zam squirmed. 'Sounds terrible. He chops it up with a knife?'

Abdul nodded.

'Sounds like hard work.'

'It is. I think Dad wants me to take over the business when he's too old, but he keeps complaining that I'm too short.'

'Why would he do that?'

'He spends most of his day dragging meat around. He reckons I won't even be able to lift it.'

'He's a strong man, then?'

'Very.'

'I see.'

'Why?'

'No reason,' said Zam with a smile.

'Hey, everyone!' shouted Hemlin. He drew the attention of everyone in the Secret Circle. 'Watch!'

Hemlin stood still for a moment, a look of absolute joy on his face. He raised his arms above his head, which reached almost as high as the tree branches above, and he laughed.

'Go!' he yelled and he began to float above the ground.

There were gasps among the onlookers. Some took steps back and held their hands over their open mouths while others laughed and looked on in complete shock. Hemlin continued to rise into the air, his body completely straight, until his hands disappeared into the branches above.

He then spun towards the ground until his whole body was straight, and guffawed at the puzzled looks from those who were close.

Hemlin then flew in a circle around the bonfire.

There were whoops and cheers from the crowd as he swooped to the ground before rising back up again. He twisted and turned and even did a loop as he whisked around the clearing like a superhero.

'What's he doing?' muttered Abdul.

Zam laughed. 'Well, it looks as though our friend Hemlin has learnt to fly.'

Simon was more confused than amazed. Since when had the imaginary friends been able to fly? Why only reveal it now?

Something then caught his eye which drew his attention away from the flying creature. While Hemlin circled the campfire (now flapping his arms like a bird), Simon noticed small poofs of dirt rise up from the ground directly below where he flew.

While all eyes were on Hemlin, Simon ran his hand down the tree stump and fumbled around on the ground. He felt for a twig and, grabbing it between two fingers, brought it slowly up to his lap.

Hemlin flew past again and the little dirt clouds burst up. As he passed, Simon threw the twig into the path of the flying creature. Hemlin soared around Secret Circle once more against the sound of children and imaginary friends laughing and whooping in delight. The creature flew back in front of Simon and directly over the twig he had thrown.

Simon had been the only one to notice it snap.

Chapter Eighteen

Simon made it home at half past five and found out it was a lot harder to climb up through the window than it was to climb down. He managed to scramble up the tree and onto the thatched roof and then shimmy his way up to the open window.

Once inside, he took off his muddy socks and hid them in the bottom of his wardrobe. As he fell into bed and pulled the covers over himself Simon could just hear the faint click of Amie's door as she too went back to bed.

'Kids, up!' was the next thing Simon heard, and a long, tiring day began.

***

The morning went as expected. PE was first, and Simon barely had enough energy to hold a tennis racquet, never mind hit a ball in the right direction with it. After that was maths and, after staring at a times table test for five minutes, Simon learnt it was possible to fall asleep with your eyes open.

During morning break Simon played football with Abdul and David. Abdul was sluggish and half-hearted, but would occasionally blast the ball in the wrong direction so David had to chase after it.

'Is there going to be another meeting tonight?' he asked when David was too far away to hear.

'I don't know,' said Simon.

David kicked the ball back and Abdul wildly sliced the ball in the wrong direction.

'Abdul!' groaned David.

'Sorry!' he yelled before lowering his voice. 'I was lucky my dad didn't catch me this morning. I was just going in through the back door when he was going out the front!'

Simon didn't say anything. He could see Lindsay Evans and Becky Walker glaring at them from across the playground.

That afternoon Simon stayed awake, but only just. Abdul sat next to him during double history and was scorned countless times by Mrs Ramsworth for talking. Simon realised how the others must have felt when he asked them all of those questions.

At the end of the day Simon managed to slip quickly out of the classroom while Abdul was kept back for having been warned about talking. After climbing into the back of his mum's car Simon put his head back against the headrest and closed his eyes, and when he next opened them they were pulling up outside the house.

Helen had obviously not found out that either of her children had snuck out the night before, as she was in a surprisingly good mood. She ordered them all a takeaway and in forty-five minutes they were eating pepperoni pizza and chicken wings while watching a cheesy action film.

Too bad Simon missed the end.

Amie, however, saw the end and even watched the evening news afterwards. At half past nine she made her way up to bed while Simon still lay sleeping on the sofa.

'Simon?'

Simon opened his eyes. 'Mm?'

'Time for bed.'

'Okay.'

Simon stretched and his bones clicked. His neck was stiff from the awkward angle he had slept in. He sat on the edge of the sofa and watched his mum close the curtains. It had started to rain and the drops patted against the windowpane.

'Listen,' said Helen. She sat on the sofa beside

Simon and put her arm tightly around him. 'I know something is bothering you at the moment; you don't need to be a psychic to figure that out. I want you to know that your dad and I are here for you, even if you do hate us for punishing you. It's only because we love you, okay?'

Simon nodded. 'I know,' he said, and he headed upstairs to get ready for bed.

***

As Simon climbed into bed the rain pounded onto the roof above. A bright flash was immediately followed by a deafening thunderclap and the rain only got heavier.

Simon looked at the clock; it was approaching ten. The constant drumming of rain on the roof was relaxing and it didn't take long for Simon to close his eyes and drift off to sleep. He didn't want to have to go to a Secret Circle meeting tonight; the warmth of his bed was far too comfortable for him to even consider getting out of it.

Even the crash of thunder overhead couldn't disturb his rest. It was just too warm, too comfortable, too cosy.

'Oi,' came an unwelcome voice though the darkness. 'I need a word.'

Despite the warmth, the comfort and the cosiness, Simon opened his eyes and was suddenly wide awake.

'Hello,' said Kannon who was perched on the edge of the bed.

'Kannon,' said Simon. 'Not tonight.'

The creature smiled. 'Oh, I agree. It's far too wet out there. We wouldn't even be able to light the fire.'

'Oh, right,' said Simon as he propped himself up onto his elbows. He hadn't expected that response. 'So, what are you doing here?'

Kannon swivelled on the bed and stretched out beside Simon. He rested his oversized hands behind his head and made Simon shuffle over until his leg almost hung out.

'Oh, you know,' said Kannon. 'I just fancied a chat, really.'

'Okay,' said Simon. 'What about?'

'I don't know. I hear your dad has gone away on business again.'

Simon nodded.

'Where's he gone?'

'London.'

'I see. He works for a bank, doesn't he?'

'Yeah.'

'What does he do there?'

Simon shrugged. 'He looks after people's accounts.'

'What people?'

'Rich people, I think.'

'I see. What is in their accounts?'

'Money.'

'Ah, all right, then. When is your dad back?'

'I don't know. Why?'

'No reason. So I heard Abdul's dad is a butler.'

Simon chuckled. 'A butcher.'

'I see. And they chop up meat to sell to people?'

'Yeah.'

'So he is a well-built man?'

Simon had seen him a few times when he dropped Abdul off at school. 'I suppose,' he said.

'Right.'

There was a moment of silence.

'Why do you want to know?' asked Simon.

'Just curious. Do you know your next-door neighbours at all?'

'Not really. They work away a lot, I think.'

'What do they do?'

'I don't know.'

'Are they away now?'

'I don't know,' said Simon rather abruptly. He should have been the one asking the questions, not the other way around.

'What about your neighbours on the other side?'

'I don't kno—'

There was a sharp knock on the bedroom door and it was pushed open from the hallway. It was his mum, and she opened the door too far and it cracked loudly.

'We really need to sort this door out,' she said with a roll of her eyes. 'Is everything okay, darling?'

Simon stared at his mum with wide eyes.

'What's the matter?' she said.

He looked to where Kannon had been lying and saw an empty space.

'Nothing,' he said.

'You're nearly falling out of bed; move yourself over a little.'

Simon shuffled his body a little further into the middle of the bed.

'G'night darling,' she said.

'Night, Mum.'

She closed the door and Simon waited till her footsteps reached the bottom of the stairs.

'Kannon?'

Nothing.

'Kannon?'

The creature didn't return.

CHAPTER NINETEEN

During morning lessons Simon actually felt awake. In science he was able to conduct electricity through various metals and in woodwork he made a nice wooden rack to store his video games, all without even a yawn. He felt refreshed and it seemed as though others from the Secret Circle felt the same; by mid-morning break nobody had been sent to Mr Cricklewood's office.

Jonathon and Jake even called Simon over to talk, and not once did any of them even hint at the Secret Circle or the imaginary friends. Simon knew that if he wanted them to stay in a good mood then he should just try to pretend that none of it ever happened.

David ran across from around the back of the assembly hall and for once Simon and the others didn't have to awkwardly change their conversation.

'Have any of you seen Abdul today?'

'Not yet,' said Jake.

'Is he not in?' asked Jonathon.

'Don't know,' said David. 'I suppose not.'

The bell then rang and they parted ways. Simon had double English before lunch. For the first hour they were looking at poetry, and it was then that Simon felt the first yawn of the day start to build.

Simon was sitting beside Jonathon at the back of the classroom and both were feeling the tiring effects of eighteenth-century poetry.

'Hey!' yelled a girl known as Kay from the desk in front. She spun around and glowered at Simon and Jonathon.

'What is it, Miss Humphreys?' said Mrs Ramsworth at the front of the classroom.

Kay turned back and grabbed the back of her head. Her ponytail flicked round and nearly hit Simon in the face.

'One of those two just threw something at me,' she moaned.

'We did not!' Jonathon yelped. He was far more awake now.

'You did! I felt it!' Kay bent over and she fumbled around on the floor before shooting her hand up in the air. 'Here, see! They threw a pencil at me!'

'Mr Turner, Mr Andrews,' growled Mrs Ramsworth

as she edged menacingly toward the back table. 'Is this true?'

'No way,' said Simon. Jonathon shook his head frantically.

Mrs Ramsworth squinted at them over the top of her glasses and Simon felt a cold wave wash over his skin. It seemed that Mrs Ramsworth had somehow now developed psychic powers as a form of punishment.

'Don't do it again,' she breathed before heading back to the front of the classroom to continue her analysis of an old poem.

Simon turned to Jonathon and kept his voice as low as it would go. 'Was that you?'

Jonathon shook his head and his cheeks wobbled. 'No, I thought it was you.'

'Since when would I do something like that?'

Jonathon shrugged. 'Maybe you fancy her or something.'

'Don't be daft!'

'Ow!' Kay's head had jolted back and her scream drew looks from the entire room, especially Mrs Ramsworth.

'What on earth is going on back there?'

Kay rubbed the back of her neck and struggled to fight back tears. 'They pulled on my ponytail.'

'Did they now?'

'No!' Simon and Jonathon answered together.

'Looks like there'll be two students missing out on their lunch break today.'

***

Simon rested his chin on his hand while Jonathon buried his head into his folded arms. The sky was surprisingly clear outside and the sound of their schoolmates in the playground made them feel even worse for being stuck inside. Mrs Ramsworth was doing some marking and had made them sit at the front of the class in silence while she thought of a suitable punishment.

'Boys, sit up!' she scorned. Simon let his arm drop to the desk but Jonathon was in no rush to sit back in his chair.

'You will both sit there in silence until you tell me which of you pulled on Miss Humphreys' hair.'

Simon and Jonathon looked at one another, and then back at Mrs Ramsworth.

'Have it your way,' she said. She slipped her glasses off her hooked nose and placed them down on the desk. 'I'm going to the headmaster's office for a moment. I hope one of you has an answer for me when I return.'

Once Mrs Ramsworth had closed the door Simon turned to Jonathon.

'Did you do it?'

'No, I didn't. You were looking at me when Kay started screaming. How could I have done it? It wasn't either of us; she's just trying to get us into trouble.'

'Okay, I'll admit it,' said Kannon, who was suddenly sitting in Mrs Ramsworth's chair. 'It was me. Funny though, wasn't it?'

'No,' said Simon.

'We're missing lunch now,' said Jonathon. 'I'm starving.'

Kannon hopped from Mrs Ramsworth's chair and sauntered over to them. 'Oh come on, it is actually quite funny. Where's your sense of humour gone?'

'What are you doing here?' said Simon. 'Someone's going to see you.'

Kannon snatched Mrs Ramsworth's glasses from her desk and held them to his face. His eyes appeared even bigger through the frames. 'She's a bit of a nasty old crone, that teacher of yours, isn't she? I know Jonathon has said she's horrible but I didn't think she'd actually be that bad.'

'Kannon, what are you doing here?'

'I bet she sits at home all alone and talks to her cats. She looks like a sad old cat woman, don't you think?' The creature laughed and jumped up to sit on the desk.

'Kannon?' said Simon.

The creature looked at him.

'What are you doing here?'

'Just saying hello. I wanted to check in on you boys, see how you are.'

'But I thought you'd never be seen anywhere during the day?' said Jonathon. 'Does this mean all the other rules have changed as well?'

'Of course not,' said Kannon. 'But you don't need to worry, I've been very careful. Is this what you boys do all day? Very boring, isn't it?'

'I–'

'Simon, is your dad back from his trip yet?'

'No, w–'

'Listen, I need to let you know something. There's going to be a very special meeting of the Secret Circle tonight, so you boys need to make sure you're in your rooms for eleven o'clock, okay? It's going to be an early one tonight.'

'Why?'

'Well if I told you now it wouldn't be very special, would it? You'll just have to wait until tonight.'

The door to the classroom opened and Kannon vanished from sight. The glasses he had been holding fell to the floor and one of the round lenses popped out of the frame.

'Have you two gentlemen had time to think about being honest while I was away?'

Simon and Jonathon said nothing; they were both too concerned about the broken glasses which lay in the middle of the floor.

CHAPTER TWENTY

That night Simon headed to bed at eight o'clock. There was little to do at home anyway, so bed seemed like the best choice.

Mr Cricklewood had telephoned Simon's mum while she was at work to tell her that either her son or Jonathon Turner had broken Mrs Ramsworth's glasses and tugged on Kay Humphrey's ponytail. Even though there was no proof it had been Simon, he had been banned from television for a week. Add to that, his video games had been taken away and he was grounded, so there was nothing else Simon could do other than sit and wait for Kannon to arrive.

He lay on top of the covers, his warm clothes already on, and he watched the clock slowly tick by.

Eight-thirty.

Nine.

Nine-thirty.

Ten.

Ten thirty.

Ten forty-five…

The clock slowed down to a crawl and Simon grew restless. During his clock watch he heard Amie go to bed, then go to the toilet, then go downstairs to get a glass of water. Then his mum went to bed, got up to answer her phone, headed back to bed, and the lights in the house finally went off for good at about ten to eleven.

As the final minutes until eleven o'clock counted down Simon decided he was fed up with lying on the bed, so he opened his curtains and looked out over the village of Hedgely. It was another cloudy night, but at least it wasn't raining, and the air was cool but calm.

'It's nice to see you're ready.'

Kannon had appeared by the door.

'Hi, Kannon.'

'Let's go.'

***

Instead of heading straight to the Secret Circle Kannon led Simon in the direction of the village hall. It was a rarely-used building, usually only opened for special events or the occasional Cub Scout or Beavers meeting. It was tucked in just behind the small pub at the opposite end of the village to where they usually entered the woods.

Simon followed Kannon down a small alleyway and they came out just outside Ryan's house, where Amie and Grork were already waiting. Amie was wearing her coat and was holding on tightly to the creature's hand.

A minute later Ryan came around from the back of the house, followed closely by Thump. The dumpy imaginary friend had a gleeful look on his podgy face.

'Only just managed to get out,' whispered Ryan as they moved on through the village. My sister nearly caught me. I think she would have if she didn't have her headphones on.'

Their next stop was Will's house. Rane was already outside and, once Will joined them, they headed to the next street to meet Jonathon, who was waiting beside Hemlin.

'That's everyone,' said Thump.

'Good,' said Kannon. 'Let's head to the Secret Circle.'

CHAPTER TWENTY-ONE

The group arrived at the woodland clearing and were greeted by the others who had been waiting for them. Lindsey Evans, Claire Ruttle and Becky Walker were standing with their imaginary friends and Warren and Jake were sitting on tree stumps with theirs.

Simon couldn't see Abdul anywhere.

The fire was crackling and a column of grey smoke was rising up into the cloud-cluttered sky. Kannon motioned for everyone to take a seat on one of the surrounding stumps.

'Thank you for coming,' announced Kannon. 'Tonight is a night where we must reveal something very important to you.'

Excited chatter around the circle was stifled as Kannon raised his hands above his head.

'Tonight will be the last meeting of the Secret Circle,

as it currently stands,' he continued. 'We can't tell you why just yet, but I can assure you it is very exciting indeed. Things will change, but it will most certainly be for the better.'

'How?' asked Becky Walker.

'You will see,' said Kannon. 'Plus, we wouldn't want to spoil the surprise. You'll start to see a few new things tomorrow, so look out for them; they'll be fun.'

'Will we see you again?' asked Jake.

'You will,' said Kannon. He smiled widely and revealed his needle-sharp teeth. 'I guarantee it. Now, everybody enjoy yourselves!'

There was confusion around the circle as Kannon stepped away from the fire. Nobody was quite sure what to make of what they had just been told. It seemed a strange thing to announce to everyone without even giving them any proper details.

'Come on, everyone! Who wants to play cards?' said Ralcar with a loud clap of his fat hands.

There was only silence amongst the Circle.

Lindsey Evans raised her hand. 'Don't we get a say in this?'

'What do you mean?' said Kannon.

'You're our imaginary friends,' she said. 'So, don't we get to say what happens? If you come from our imaginations, why can't we just imagine that you stay here in the Secret Circle?'

'Yeah, what if we don't want things to change?' said Will.

'Things have to change if they want to stand the tests of time,' said the creature. 'And now is the time for that change. This has to happen, and it will happen. Please, try to have fun.'

'I don't know if I can, now,' said Claire Ruttle. 'I don't want things to change.'

'Things have always been changing. Each day has been different from the last,' said Rane. 'None of you seemed to mind before.'

'What if we did mind, but didn't say anything?' said Ryan.

'Yeah,' added Amie.

'Like what?' said Kannon.

'Where's Abdul?' said Simon.

'He decided he doesn't want to be a part of the Secret Circle anymore.'

'That's what you said about Luke when he left,' said Lindsey.

'Because there's nothing else to say. Enough of this now; everybody have fun.'

It had certainly been a struggle for anybody to have fun during what they knew to be the last meeting of the Secret Circle 'as it currently stands.' There had been no games or laughing, only saddened conversation. Most of them left early, and Simon and Amie were back at home before two o'clock.

Simon fell asleep almost straight away, but his dreams were full of the imaginary friends.

CHAPTER TWENTY-TWO

The next morning, Simon woke up with a ray of sun squeezing through a gap in the curtains which then rested on his eyes. He felt sluggish, like he'd slept all day, and his throat was dry and sticky.

Simon pushed himself up and looked at the clock. It was almost half past eight and school was due to start in twenty minutes.

Was it Saturday? He had lost track of the days, but he didn't think he'd lost track that much.

No, it couldn't be Saturday; it must be Friday.

So, where was his mum? Normally she would be scrambling Simon and his sister into the car at this point.

Simon left the warmth of his bed and headed downstairs. The house was quiet and there were no signs that his mum had even been there. Usually her handbag would be on the kitchen table and she would be running around getting things ready for work and school.

'Mum?' he called out.

Simon poured himself a glass of orange juice and looked at the clock. It was twenty-five minutes to nine. They were going to be very late for school now.

Simon went back upstairs and knocked on his mum's bedroom door. 'Mum?'

There was no reply.

Simon pushed open the door and poked his head inside. The bedcovers were in a ball on the floor and the lamp on the bedside table had fallen onto its side.

'Mum?' he said again, but she wasn't there.

Simon crossed the hall and knocked on his sister's door.

'Yeah?' she mumbled.

'Amie, it's me, can I come in?'

'Okay.'

Simon pushed open the door and saw his sister sitting up, clutching her stuffed bear. She rubbed her eyes and yawned.

'Is it time for school?' she said.

'It should be,' said Simon. 'But I can't find Mum anywhere.'

'Maybe she went out to the shops.'

Simon pulled open the curtains and looked out onto

the street below. His mum's car was still parked on the road.

'Her car's still there.'

'Ring her phone. Maybe she went for a walk.'

Simon ran downstairs and into the living room. The house phone, which was usually on the small table beside the sofa, was gone.

'Amie, where's the phone?' he shouted.

'Don't know,' she called back.

Simon put on his trainers, grabbed his coat, and opened the front door. There was a coating of frost on the front garden, and the whole village was still. Usually Simon would hear something – either a passing car or the droning of a leaf blower.

This morning the village was silent.

Simon ran out into the street. 'Mum?'

'Simon, what's going on?' Amie had appeared at the front door, her stuffed bear still in her arms.

'Amie, go inside,' he said. 'Close the door and go back to your bedroom. I'll be back in a minute.'

'Okay,' she said. 'Hurry.'

Simon jogged through the village. Where he was going he wasn't quite sure; he just hoped he'd bump into somebody who had seen his mum. There were more cars in the village than usual. Hadn't anybody driven to work that morning?

'Mum!' he shouted again.

'Hello?' a faint voice called back.

'Mum?'

'Who's that?'

It wasn't his mum, but Simon recognised the voice.

'Jonathon?'

'Yeah. Who is it?'

'It's Simon. Where are you?'

Simon ran into the next street and the voice grew louder. 'Here.'

Simon groaned. 'Where's here?'

'Near Ryan's house.'

Simon passed through the alley by the village hall and emerged in the next street. Cars lined the side of the road, and there were no other signs of life except for Jonathon, who stood in his dressing gown holding a banana.

'What are you doing here?' said Simon.

'I can't find my gran anywhere,' he said. 'Sometimes she goes for tea at Mr and Mrs Jenkins' house, but they're not in either. Then I went to see if Mr Pennywhistle was home, but he must be in bed or out or something, because he didn't answer the door.'

'Have you not seen all the cars around here? How could they have gone anywhere without those?'

'I don't know,' admitted Jonathon.

'Simon?'

Ryan had appeared at his bedroom window.

'Jonathon? What are you doing here?'

'Are your parents home?' said Simon.

'I assume so. I know my sister is, I can hear her in the shower.'

'Have you looked for them?'

'No, why?'

'My grandma isn't home,' said Jonathon.

'Neither are my parents,' added Simon.

'Where are they?'

'If we knew that we wouldn't be here looking for them,' said Jonathon.

'They're not in there with your mum and dad, are they?'

'Hang on, I'll check.' Ryan disappeared back inside.

Simon and Jonathon passed through the front gate and down the garden path to the front door. Ryan's house, like the others in Hedgely, was a thatched roof cottage, except this one had the outside walls painted white.

'This is a bit weird, isn't it?' said Jonathon.

'Very,' said Simon. 'Jonathon, what's the banana for?'

'Breakfast. My grandma usually peels it for me. That's why I came out looking for her.'

'You know you can peel those yourself, don't you?'

Jonathon looked at Simon like he was speaking a foreign language.

The front door opened and Ryan appeared with a look on his face which didn't give Simon much confidence.

'My parents aren't here either.'

Jonathon groaned and stamped his foot. 'Then where are they?'

'They've not gone to a meeting in the village hall or something, have they?' said Ryan.

'Wouldn't we have heard about that?' said Simon. 'I walked past it on the way here anyway; it looked shut to me.'

'Then what's going on, where are they?' said Jonathon.

Ryan looked at Simon, who could only shrug.

'Try calling them,' said Jonathon.

'I couldn't find my phone at home,' said Simon.

'Let's try ours,' said Ryan. Simon and Jonathon followed Ryan into the house and through to the living room. The walls and carpet were all a neutral beige colour, but the furniture was dark. Simon and Jonathon sat on the deep red sofa while Ryan scoured the room.

'I can't find it,' said Ryan. 'It's not in here.'

'Where is it usually?' said Jonathon.

'On the mantelpiece,' said Ryan. He pointed to the

marble fireplace, and above the old coals was a shelf lined with cat ornaments. There was a space on one side where the phone should have been.

'Are there any more phones in the house?' said Simon.

Ryan shook his head. After a moment his face brightened. 'Rachel has one.'

He darted from the living room and stood at the bottom of the stairs.

'Rachel!'

There was no reply from upstairs, but something clattered loudly.

'Rachel!'

Footsteps thudded in the room above the living room and a door opened hard.

'What?' came a screech.

'Can I use your mobile?'

'No.'

The door slammed shut.

Ryan slumped back into the living room.

'I don't think that's an option at the minute,' he said. He flopped into the chair beside the window and sighed.

'So, what now?' said Jonathon.

'Have you seen Will yet?' said Ryan.

'Not yet,' said Simon.

'I came straight here,' said Jonathon.

'Maybe we should go see if he's there?'

'And see if his parents aren't?' said Simon.

Ryan nodded. 'Yeah, I suppose.'

The trio stood up and headed out of the living room. As Ryan pulled open the front door there was another loud crash from upstairs, followed by more thundering footsteps.

'Ryan!' came a scream from upstairs. The door was yanked open again. 'Ryan!'

Ryan rolled his eyes. 'What?'

More heavy footsteps, this time moving along the hallway and finally onto the stairs.

'What have you done with my phone?' said Rachel, who emerged wearing only a towel over her body and another wrapped around her head. She was glaring at her brother, but then she spotted Simon and Jonathon standing in the doorway to the living room. 'Why are you lot here? What time is it?'

Simon and Jonathon shuffled awkwardly. Rachel was certainly a beautiful girl, and to see her standing there in just a towel left them unsure where to look.

'It's nearly nine o'clock. Mum and Dad aren't here,' said Ryan.

'They'll be at work,' said Rachel.

'Well they didn't wake me up, they didn't take me to school first, did they?'

'And the car's outside,' said Simon.

Rachel looked at Simon, then back at her brother. 'Whatever, where's my phone?'

'I haven't seen it.'

'Well, it was on my desk when I went to bed last night; where is it now?'

'Rachel, I haven't touched your phone. The house phone has gone as well.'

'What?' Rachel came the rest of the way downstairs and barged past Simon and Jonathon. Simon was sure he saw Jonathon's cheeks turn red. 'Where is it?'

'We don't know that either.'

Rachel groaned and pushed past Simon and Jonathon again. Jonathon cleared his throat loudly.

'I'm going to get dressed,' said Rachel as she stormed back upstairs.

'What are we supposed to do till then?' said Ryan.

'I don't care,' said Rachel and she slammed her bedroom door shut again.

'I think I should stay here,' said Ryan. You guys go and see if Will's at home.'

Simon nodded. 'We'll meet you back here.'

'Okay,' said Ryan. 'Don't be long.'

Chapter Twenty-Three

Will lived on the next road along but there was no connecting alleyway, so Simon and Jonathon had to walk along toward the village green. The village was still silent – even the birds weren't chirping.

Jonathon still held on to his banana. Simon even offered to peel it for him but it seemed Jonathon wasn't that hungry any more.

'Guys!'

Simon and Jonathon stopped and listened.

'Guys, here!'

Will was on the other side of the village green. He was bolting toward them, first across the bridge that spanned the stream, then across the grass of the green itself. He looked panicked and his face closely resembled a tomato.

'Don't tire yourself out too much,' shouted Jonathon. 'You don't want to be the first eleven-year-old to have a heart attack.'

'Run!' he yelled back.

'What?'

'Run!'

Jonathon's smile dropped and he looked at Simon.

Will suddenly flipped to the side and somersaulted into the air, his arms and legs flailing uncontrollably. He managed to scream before hitting the ground hard on his front.

Simon didn't think, he just ran to help Will while Jonathon stood looking dumbfounded.

Will managed to raise his head. 'Stop! Don't come over here!'

Simon didn't listen. As he reached the edge of the green Jonathon screamed from behind and he too was catapulted to the side. He flipped and landed on his bottom on the bonnet of a red car, which dented under the force.

'What's happening?' yelled Simon. He was glued to the spot, waiting for his own feet to leave the ground right in the middle of where Will and Jonathon were groaning in pain.

'It's them,' said Will.

'Who?' said Simon. He spun on the spot but could see nothing at all out of the ordinary.

'Them.' Will was pointing behind Simon, and he

turned again to see the grinning face of Kannon looking back at him.

'Hello, Simon,' said the creature.

'What are you doing?' said Simon.

'Just having a little fun,' said Kannon. 'Something you seem to struggle with, yourself.'

'*This* is fun?'

'Very,' said Grork, who had appeared from behind. He had a small smile spread across his fat lips. 'Think of it as the kind of fun a kid who burns ants using a magnifying glass would have.'

'Satisfying,' added Kannon.

'But it's not fun for us,' said Simon.

'That doesn't matter anymore.' Thump had appeared on the other side, and Simon was now surrounded by the creatures.

'Of course it matters,' said Simon. 'If you're our imaginary friends, then do what I imagine. I don't think anybody would have imagined this.'

'Come on, Simon,' said Kannon. 'You, the one with all the questions, still believe that?'

'I never believed it,' said Simon.

Kannon chuckled. 'I knew you would be a problem. Good thing we had everything set before you joined the Secret Circle.'

'Everything set for what?'

'Our takeover.'

Jonathon groaned. 'Simon, what's he talking about?'

'Shut up, fatty,' said Kannon. 'Let someone with a little sense do the talking.'

'Don't talk to him like that,' said Simon. He could feel his heart drumming, and the adrenalin was making him say things he probably should have kept to himself.

'You're feisty,' said Kannon. 'I like that. It's a good quality to have. I'm going to be very disappointed when we kill you.'

Simon couldn't think of any words to say other than, 'What?'

'Yes, it is a sad reality we have to face at some point, but all of you will die in the very near future, as soon as you're done being useful.'

'Simon!' called a voice from nearby.

It was Ryan.

He had emerged at the end of his street with his sister, who was now dressed in a white top and jeans, though her hair was wet and stringy. She had stopped and was staring open-mouthed at the creatures.

'What are they?' she said.

Kannon was staring at Ryan, a malicious look in his glassy eyes. 'Oh look, now we have less work to do. Grork,

138

Thump, fetch them to me.'

The two oddly-sized creatures passed Simon and strode towards Ryan and Rachel.

'Run!' yelled Simon.

'There's no point in running,' said Kannon. 'We'll catch you.'

Suddenly the silence throughout the village was filled with the sound of a revving car engine. Grork and Thump stopped and the three imaginary friends turned to face the other side of the village green. A car rounded the corner and turned into the road which ran alongside the stream.

It was Brian's car.

'Ah, it looks like we missed one. Come on boys, we can finish this later.'

The three creatures vanished.

'Where are they?' said Ryan.

'I don't know,' said Simon. He was staring at his dad's car as it pulled up outside the house and the sound of the engine died.

'What are those things?' said Rachel, but nobody answered.

Simon saw a splash in the stream and he immediately broke into a run. His heart was drumming harder and faster and sweat was already streaking across his forehead.

'Dad!' he yelled.

Brian saw his son bolting across the village green. He opened the car door and climbed out.

'Simon? Why aren't you at sch–'

Brian started squirming uncomfortably and his voice muffled while he tried to speak. His legs kicked out and his arms were held tight against his body. His whole body went rigid, but his eyes were wide open and flicking back and forth.

'Dad!' Simon cried again. As Simon reached the street Brian began floating back toward the village green, his body straight and still.

Simon felt a dull pain in his chest and he fell to the ground gasping for breath. He tried to call out to his dad, but the air in his body had gone and all he could manage was a weak cough.

The only thing Simon could do was lie on the road and watch as his dad's twitching body floated across the village green and disappeared into a nearby street.

CHAPTER TWENTY-FOUR

It took ten minutes for Simon to regain control of his breathing. His chest ached with every breath he took and he had scraped his arm on the road when he fell, which stung as he ran it under the cold tap.

Simon had gone home to check on Amie, and those who remained in Hedgely were with him. Will and Ryan sat at the kitchen table while Rachel paced back and forth. Jonathon was perched on the stairs with his arms wrapped around his knees.

'How long have they been here?' said Rachel.

'I've known Hemlin three weeks,' said Jonathon.

'Just over three weeks for me,' said Will.

'Five weeks,' said Amie. She was holding on to her brother's leg while he looked out over the back garden.

'And none of you thought it was strange?' said Rachel.

None of them answered.

'None of you thought that funny creatures coming into your bedrooms at night was something you should maybe tell somebody about?'

'Do you think Mum and Dad would have believed me if I had told them?' said Ryan.

Rachel sighed. She would be the first to admit she would have thought her brother was crazy if he told her something like that.

'So, now what do we do? These things have obviously taken our parents somewhere,' she said. 'Where would they go?'

'To the woods, maybe?' said Will.

'The woods where you had your little meetings?'

They all nodded.

'Well let's try there, then,' said Rachel. 'Let's go get them.'

Ryan huffed. 'You saw what they did to Simon's dad. Made him paralysed or whatever, then levitated him. If he couldn't do anything to stop it then how can we?'

Rachel's eyes flicked back and forth. 'Weapons.'

'Like what?'

'I don't know, knives, hammers, cricket bats... anything you can swing and do some damage with.'

'I think my dad has an axe in the shed,' said Will.

'Great,' said Rachel. 'That's what we need. You heard what that thing said. If they plan on killing us then we need to do something right now.'

'I'll check our shed as well,' said Simon. 'I'm sure there'll be something in there.'

Rachel nodded. 'Everybody go check your sheds. We need as many weapons as we can grab if we're going to fight these things.'

Amie held on more tightly to her brother's leg and let out a quiet whimper.

'We need to stay in groups,' said Simon, putting his hand on Amie's back.

'Yeah, Ryan and I will go to our house and see what we can find, so Jonathon and Will, you go to your houses and grab whatever you can.'

Jonathon moaned. 'How are we supposed to fight those things? They flung me ten feet in the air; we can't do anything.'

'So what are you going to do, sit and wait for them to kill you?' said Ryan.

'Those things have your grandma, Jonathon. If you don't fight for her then what chance does she have?' said Simon.

Jonathon looked up. His eyes were red and puffy, and he cleared his throat and nodded.

'We need to move before they come back,' said Rachel.

'Where should we meet?' said Ryan.

'At Will's,' said Simon. 'It's closest to the Secret Circle.'

'Okay,' said Rachel. 'We'll meet at Will's house in five minutes. Let's go.'

Once the others had left, Simon went out into the back garden and rooted around in the shed which sat in the shade of the trees. There was very little of much use among the brooms and cobwebs, and he couldn't really start swinging a lawnmower over his head. The only thing he felt was useful was a pair of partly-rusted hedge clippers which, if used with enough strength, could maybe cut one of the creature's heads clean off.

Or, more likely, give them a nasty cut.

Simon went straight back inside and helped Amie put on her shoes and coat. They then left the house and raced through the village. Will and Jonathon were already waiting for them in the doorway of Will's parents' bungalow, and they made their way inside.

***

Ryan and Rachel arrived a minute after Simon and Amie and

they locked themselves inside the house. Will's parents were in the process of decorating, so the whole house already looked like a building site. The living room carpet had been removed, revealing the old wooden floorboards underneath. The furniture had been pushed away from the walls and had been draped in sheets of various colours. Pots of paint were stacked in piles around the room and the walls had been freshly layered with strong-smelling plaster.

Will pulled the curtains closed and they sat with the lights off, trying their best to keep their voices quiet.

'All I could find were these,' said Simon. He showed the others the hedge clippers. 'Better than nothing.'

'We found these,' said Rachel. She held up a wooden pole which had a long, sharp, curved blade on one end. 'It's a scythe.'

'And I have this,' said Ryan. He was holding an air rifle and had a box of pellets in his pocket. 'Sometimes me and Dad shoot cans at the end of the garden. He'd kill me if he knew I took it.'

Simon looked at Will and Jonathon. 'What did you get?'

'I have the axe,' said Will. 'It's a bit blunt but I think it could still do some damage. Jonathon found these though.'

Jonathon put a bucket down in front of him and pulled off the sheet which had been draped on top. Inside were five small, dark sticks.

'What are they?' said Rachel.

'Dynamite,' he said calmly.

Others around the room gasped.

'My grandad had them to blow up old tree stumps in the garden. They're not like the dynamite you see in films but they can still make a mess if you're too close.'

'Oh great, so we're going to start throwing bombs around the woods now?' snorted Ryan.

'Shut up, Ryan,' said Rachel. 'It's better than nothing. But maybe I should look after them. When we find them, I don't want my dad going bonkers knowing I let you carry dynamite around. Well, if we do find them.'

'If?' said Amie. She sniffed loudly.

'When,' corrected Simon. 'When we find them. They can't have gone far. I bet they're in the middle of the Secret Circle right now.'

'With Ryan's gun we can probably pick those things off without even getting close,' said Jonathon.

'You trust my brother to shoot around your grandma?' said Rachel. 'When he told you he shoots tin cans he didn't tell you he doesn't actually hit them.'

Jonathon looked away from Rachel and his cheeks glowed red.

'Oi, I'm not a bad shot,' said Ryan, raising his voice

a little too much.

'Shh,' said Will. 'You'll give away our position.'

'They probably already know where we are,' said Jonathon. 'They turned up at school the other day when me and Simon were in detention at school.'

'Me too,' said Ryan. 'I was in the toilet when Randall showed up.'

'And me,' said Will. 'Thump showed up in the garden when I got home from school.'

'Did they tell you about the Secret Circle meeting?' said Simon.

'Yeah,' said Ryan. 'Randall kept going on about how it was a special meeting.'

'There was nothing special about last night,' said Jonathon. 'It was depressing. I didn't want things to change.'

While they spoke, the soft sound of hissing filled the room.

'Well I guess this is the change,' said Ryan. 'Kidnapping our parents and trying to kill us. Nice change, eh.'

The hissing grew louder.

'What's that noise?' said Will.

They stopped and listened but none of them could quite make out where the sound was coming from. It was like a gas leak, high-pitched and steady.

Amie then whimpered and pointed at the wooden floor by Rachel's feet. One of the small sticks of dynamite was fizzling beside the bucket.

'Oh my god,' uttered Rachel. 'Everybody run!'

There was a desperate scramble as they poured out of the room. Rachel had managed to grab the bucket of dynamite, and slammed the door behind her as she followed the others out. Will fumbled with the keys on the front door.

'Hurry!'

'Come on, Will!'

'Open the door!'

Crack.

The whole group braced themselves. Simon had expected the walls to explode and a ball of fire to blow out the door, but the sound from the room next door was more like a dodgy firework than a stick of dynamite.

'Was that it?' said Ryan.

'Well, I did say it wasn't like in films,' said Jonathon. 'Put that inside a tree stump, though, and it would blow it to pieces.'

Rachel pressed down the handle on the living room door and carefully pushed it open. There was a hole in the middle of the floor and the stench of smoke was thick in the air. The furniture had been blown back against the walls and the pots of paint had burst over the entire room, even coating the cracked glass of the windows.

'See, it did some damage,' said Jonathon.

But something else had caught Simon's eye. He could see Zam, covered in white paint, slouched in the corner of the room.

Chapter Twenty-Five

'Is that one of those things?' said Rachel.

'Yeah,' said Simon. 'That's Zam. He was Claire's imaginary friend.'

'How did he get in here?' said Will. 'The doors and windows were all shut.'

'We don't know what these things can do,' said Ryan.

'Hemlin can even fly, remember,' said Jonathon. 'So Zam could have come in through the keyhole or anything.'

The creature groaned and rolled onto its back. The white paint had blasted his head and upper body, and the scar on his face was speckled with fresh blood.

'He's waking up,' said Jonathon.

Zam groaned again and Amie whimpered.

'Do something,' she shrieked.

Rachel grabbed the creature's limp arm. 'Simon,

help me lift it. Ryan, go and get some rope from the shed. Hurry.'

Ryan bolted from the room as Simon lifted Zam's other arm and helped Rachel drag the creature onto the sofa. Its head lolled back and forth as it groaned again.

Ryan skidded back into the living room, and he and his sister wrapped the creature tightly in the rope. Ryan had been to a few of the Cub Scout meetings in the village hall, so he was good with tying tight knots.

'Now what?' said Will.

'No idea, but at least he can't hurt anyone,' said Rachel.

'How do you know that?' said Jonathon. 'They made Simon's dad fly ten minutes ago. For all you know he could shoot lasers out of his eyes or burn through the rope.'

Rachel was stuck for words.

Zam groaned again and tried to stretch out his arms. His big, round eyes flicked open and, as he realised there was a crowd around him, he screamed and tried to force his arms free.

'What are you doing? Let me go!' he yelled.

Then the creature's arms and legs disappeared.

Everybody took a step back and gasped.

'See, what's it doing now?' cried Jonathon.

'His arms fell off!' said Will.

Zam's face and upper body were still visible, albeit masked under the white paint. A moment later the creature's arms and legs came back before disappearing once again.

Simon waved his hand at the empty space where Zam's leg had been and his hand hit something that wasn't there.

'They can make themselves invisible,' said Simon. 'They're not imaginary. They can't just do things we think of – they just make themselves invisible.'

'Shut up!' snarled Zam. He was still writhing and moaning as he tried to loosen the rope.

'They can do anything,' said Jonathon. 'We saw it. Hemlin flew and they made your dad fly as well. They do whatever they want!'

'Hemlin didn't fly,' said Simon.

'Quiet!' Zam screeched.

'It was just Grork carrying him. Grork was invisible so it just looked like Hemlin was flying. You could see his footsteps on the ground. It was the same with my dad. They all just grabbed him when they were invisible so it looked like he was floating. That's why his legs disappear but we can see his face. His body might be invisible but we can still see it through the paint.'

'Shut up!'

'Is that how it all works?' demanded Rachel.

Zam snarled, showing his thin, pointy teeth.

'So that's how they can sneak into the house,' said Will. 'They just wander in all invisible then, when it's time, they show themselves.'

'How long had you been waiting in here, Zam?' said Simon.

Zam screamed and spat thick spittle across the room.

'I don't think he's going to talk,' said Ryan.

'There's nothing for me to hide, now,' hissed the creature. 'Whatever happens, we've won. Your ridiculous little lives are over.'

'What have you won?' said Simon. 'Where are our parents?'

'We've won your village,' said Zam. 'It's ours now. We've claimed it as our own. Your parents are just the cost of our operation.'

'What are you talking about?' said Ryan.

'Why does an imaginary friend need an operation?' said Jonathon.

Zam laughed and tugged at the rope. 'You are a funny one, Jonathon. We're not imaginary. We don't come from inside your heads. We're as real as any of you are; we just come from somewhere different to you, that's all.'

'Where?' said Simon.

'Another world,' said Zam.

There were some confused looks around the room.

'What do you mean?' said Rachel.

'I don't know how it works,' said Zam. 'But somehow our world is connected to yours and we found a way to go between them.'

'How?' said Simon.

'Through a Gateway. I don't know where it came from or why, but it means we can just walk through it in our world and then come out in yours.'

'That doesn't make sense,' said Will.

'Things don't have to make sense to be real,' said Zam.

'I don't trust him,' said Rachel. 'They've lied before, they can lie again.'

'Then that's up to you,' spat Zam. 'Not that it matters. You'll all be dead soon anyway, and we'll have this place to ourselves.'

'Why do you want our village?' said Ryan.

'In our world there are creatures faster, taller, angrier and stronger than anything you have ever seen. They have more teeth, more eyes and more legs. There are things that could trample you, eat you, crush you or snap you. It's hard living in a world where you're food for everything else. That's why we want to come here. Here, we can be the ones who do the eating.'

'So why do you need to kill us?' said Jonathon.

'We've seen what you humans can do. You kill and maim each other all the time, so I doubt you would be keen to have guests in a world you rule. If we do things one step at a time, then becoming the dominant race in this world should be simple.'

'So, our parents are already…' Will trailed off.

'Oh they're probably not dead yet, but soon enough,' said Zam. He was still squirming but his efforts were starting to weaken. 'They will make excellent bait for any beasts which try and get in our way when we make our big move into the village.'

Rachel turned to Simon. 'Can I have a word with you?'

Simon nodded and followed Rachel into the hallway. Zam was still groaning and struggling; the noise was loud as it bounced from the blank walls.

'We need to do something fast,' said Rachel. 'If what this thing is saying is true then we have to move now.'

'I don't want Amie to go,' said Simon. 'She has to stay here.'

Rachel nodded. 'Let's ask Will to stay here and watch your sister. They need to make sure that thing doesn't escape, anyway. So where do you suppose this Gateway thing is?'

Simon shook his head. 'I don't know, but I could probably guess. They took my dad toward the woods, so I bet the Gateway is in the Secret Circle.'

'Then that's where we need to go,' said Rachel.

Simon nodded. 'I just need to get one more thing.'

CHAPTER TWENTY-SIX

Will helped Simon hunt around in the back of the shed one more time.

'Here,' said Will as he bent down beneath an old garden umbrella.

He pulled out a water pistol and handed it to Simon.

'Any more?' said Simon.

Will rifled around again and managed to find two more. They looked more like bright yellow machine guns than water pistols, but Simon knew they would be perfect for what he had in mind.

Back inside the house Simon managed to find a pot of light blue paint which had escaped the blast. He poured it into the reservoir, and then pumped the gun a few times until the pressure inside made it stiff.

'What are you doing?' said Jonathon.

'Paint made Zam show up, so why wouldn't it do

the same for the others?' said Simon.

'Of course,' said Rachel excitedly. 'If these things can turn invisible then covering them in paint from the water guns will mean we can always see them. If we can see them, then that takes away their advantage.'

'I'm pretty sure my gun can do more damage than those things,' said Ryan.

'How can you do damage if you can't even see what you're shooting at?' said Simon. 'Look.'

Simon sprayed Zam's legs with blue paint. Zam struggled and groaned. As he faded from visible to invisible his legs stayed bright and blue in full view.

'See,' said Simon. 'If we can see them, then we can shoot them.'

Ryan nodded. 'So let's go, then.'

***

Will agreed to stay at home and watch over Amie and Zam while the others headed outside. Simon, Jonathon and Rachel each had a paint-loaded water pistol while Ryan held tight onto the air rifle. A box of pellets rattled in his pocket, and Jonathon had to make do with putting his banana in his own pocket.

Rachel had taken the four remaining sticks of dynamite and wrapped each in a plastic sandwich bag. She had found a lighter in a kitchen drawer and packed them all carefully in one of Ryan's old backpacks, which she had fastened tightly to her shoulder.

The village was still silent and a covering of autumn cloud stretched across the sky. The only movement for miles around was the gentle swaying of the surrounding trees.

The group passed along the road by the village green. Beside the road was the car Jonathon had landed on, a deep dent imprinted on the bonnet.

'Where are we heading?' said Rachel.

'Around the back, through the alleyway,' said Simon.

Rachel hadn't been in the woods since she and her friends used to spend the day building forts out of fallen branches and ferns. Since becoming a teenager her interests had changed and now she would rather text her friends on her mobile phone than run around between the trees. To her, it was like the woods were new.

'I don't suppose they've just given up and left?' said Ryan hopefully.

'I doubt it,' said Simon. 'Zam seemed serious when he was going on about them wanting to take over the world.'

'I suppose you need to be serious about it when you decide to take over the world,' said Jonathon.

The bush beside them shook, and Jonathon dived to the side and shot like he was in an action film. Simon, Rachel and Ryan watched as Jonathon screamed and replaced the green of the bush with a deep shade of orange. A cat darted out and meowed before seeking cover beneath a car.

'Let's not start shooting cats just yet,' said Rachel with a smile.

Jonathon got back to his feet and frowned as the others laughed nervously.

'We haven't got enough paint to go round the village,' said Simon.

'Shut up,' grumbled Jonathon.

'Yeah, shut up,' said Grork who appeared from behind and swiped Rachel into the road.

Simon spun to shoot but Grork swung his arm again and batted the pistol from his hand. The bulky creature then shoved Simon in the shoulder and sent him sprawling to the ground.

Ryan pulled the trigger and a pellet zipped into Grork's shoulder. A spray of blood landed on Jonathon's pyjama top; he screamed in disgust, and then dived away from the creature over the boot of a parked car. Grork held his shoulder and glowered at Ryan, who took aim again and shot the creature in the arm.

Grork moaned and batted Ryan away. He hit a

wooden fence hard and slumped awkwardly to the floor.

'Ryan!' screeched Rachel, which drew the massive creature's attention to her.

Rachel fumbled for the water pistol which had fallen beside her. She shot at Grork but the creature ducked to the side and the stream of yellow paint splattered onto the side of a red van.

Simon managed to scramble to his feet and he leant over a car, his water pistol pointed straight at the creature. He pumped as fast as he could and, once the pressure was full, he shot the blue paint at Grork and coated his thick legs. As the creature faded his blue legs stayed visible, and as he reappeared he bellowed in anger.

Grork stopped and turned. He was between Rachel and Simon and seemed confused as to who he should go for.

A shot came from behind and the creature grabbed the back of his head. Simon could just see Ryan leaning against the wooden fence, his rifle buried into his shoulder and one eye closed as he looked down the sight.

Rachel pumped her water pistol again and sprayed the creature's side in bright yellow. Grork spun on the spot as Simon joined in with the shooting; the creature didn't know who to approach and stamped his fat feet like a spoilt child.

'Hit him again, Ryan,' screamed Jonathon. He ran

up beside Simon, pumping his water pistol. Jonathon had a cut on his forehead and a trickle of blood had already started to dry on his face.

Grork roared in frustration and pounded the ground with his fists. The earth shook and, somewhere nearby, a car alarm started blaring loudly. The creature reached out and grabbed at a green car at the side of the road. He heaved it above his head and hurled it at Ryan, who could only watch as it smashed into the side of the red van in front and then crumpled into a ball of metal. A tyre broke away and crushed the wooden fence Ryan leant against and a spray of splinters littered the ground in every direction.

'They can lift up cars now?' said Jonathon. He turned to Simon, a frantic look on his round face. 'Since when did they start throwing cars?'

'Just shoot!' screamed Simon.

Grork pounded the ground again and the smashed car bounced on the spot. The three streams of paint were now hitting the creature and he bellowed in anger as he was coated in bright, sticky liquid.

Ryan reloaded his rifle and shot Grork again, this time in the neck. The creature gargled and a spurt of red blood mingled with the orange, yellow and blue of the paint.

Grork tried to swing again but he slipped and fell heavily onto the road. He was holding tightly onto his neck, but thick red blood was still pouring from beneath his hand. The creature gargled again and twitched.

'Stop,' said Simon. He and the others stopped shooting and stood in silence. Grork was lying still, though his hand still clung to his fat neck.

'Is he dead?' said Jonathon.

'I don't think so,' said Ryan.

Rachel pumped her water pistol. 'So shoot him again. Finish him off.'

Ryan took a pellet from his pocket and managed to keep his hand steady enough so that he could slip it into the barrel of the rifle. Once in, he clicked the rifle back and rested it into his shoulder, then pointed it directly at Grork's neck.

CHAPTER TWENTY-SEVEN

'Do it!' yelled Jonathon.

Ryan held the gun tightly and, with one eye shut, he aimed.

Grork gurgled and his leg kicked the ground.

'Hurry!'

Before he could pull the trigger Ryan collapsed in a heap and let out a loud cry of pain. He held his shin and tried to scream again but no sound came out.

'Ryan?' said Rachel. She too then fell onto the road as her knees gave way.

'What is it?' said Simon as he looked frantically around.

'It's one of them,' said Rachel. 'Shoot it!'

Simon began shooting paint wildly around. He hit the road, a lamppost, a car and even Rachel, but nothing that couldn't be seen.

Simon then felt a stabbing pain in the back of his leg and he fell back into a heap. He felt something move over his mouth, and as he tried to scream he felt like he could only hear it inside his head.

He yelled to Jonathon, who was watching with wide eyes.

'MmmmHmmm!'

'What?' said Jonathon. He took a step back.

'Mmmh!'

'I don't know what you mean!'

Simon thrashed with his arm and knocked something away from his mouth.

'Shoot!'

'Oh, okay,' said Jonathon. He then sprayed paint at Simon, but missed as he hit an invisible barrier. Suddenly an orange face was hovering above Simon, a twisted look of disgust outlining the features.

'Thump!' said Jonathon.

'What?' yelled the creature. 'You can see me?'

The small face turned and looked toward the twitching figure of Grork, then turned back to Jonathon and snarled. He then bobbed off across the village green and splashed into the stream.

Simon sat up and forced himself to stand. 'Up! Quick,' he said through a grimace. 'He's washing off the paint! Run!'

Simon helped Ryan to his feet and took off after Jonathon and Rachel, who were already bolting across the green.

'Where are you going?' Simon shouted.

'I don't know,' Jonathon called back.

There was a flurry of water spurting in the stream where Thump had jumped in. His face had vanished, so the paint must have washed off, but they could just make out the outline of the stumpy creature as he splashed about in the water.

A moment later the splashing stopped.

Simon took Rachel's hand and grabbed onto the flapping sleeve of Jonathon's pyjama top. He led them quickly away as the shimmering figure of the imaginary friend began to fade away.

Simon had seen his dad's car, the driver's door still open.

'Into the car!' yelled Simon.

Jonathon dived in through the open door and scrambled into the passenger seat. Simon followed and slammed the door behind him as Rachel and Ryan leapt into the back and locked the doors.

Thump then showed himself. He was striding calmly across the green and was quickly approaching the car.

'Now what?' said Jonathon.

'I'll shoot him,' said Ryan, raising the gun up to his shoulder.

'Don't be stupid,' said Rachel, knocking the gun down. 'You'll smash the window and let him in if you do that!'

'Then use the dynamite!'

'You expect me to start throwing dynamite all over the place?'

'Well, do something!'

Thump reached the car and jumped onto the bonnet. He stopped for a second and looked inside. His face was small and the features too close together, but it was still easy to tell that he was furious.

Thump vanished and was followed by a few short seconds of silence.

Loud, deafening thuds began landing on the metal shell of the car. It was like thunder to their ears and Jonathon whined and ducked his head down.

The back windscreen cracked and a wing mirror was torn off and flung to the ground.

Across the green, Grork stood up. He steadied himself and stretched his hulking arms above his head, then turned to face the car.

There was muffled speech. Simon couldn't make out

the words, but whatever it was must have been an invitation, as Grork began bounding towards them.

'He's coming this way!' shrieked Jonathon.

'Can I shoot now?' said Ryan.

'No, drive,' said Rachel.

'What?' snapped Simon.

Rachel pointed at the keys which were still in the ignition. 'Drive!'

Grork was closer. The ground shook with each of his thundering steps.

Simon turned the key and the engine roared to life. His dad had let him drive once, in an empty supermarket car park, but that hadn't involved a chase with any murderous monsters. He sort of knew what he had to do to get it moving, so he pushed the clutch pedal down with his left foot and slipped the gear stick into first gear.

'Go!' screeched Jonathon. He was unable to take his eyes from Grork, who was so close he could make out the enraged look in the creature's eyes.

Simon slammed his foot onto the accelerator pedal and the car jolted, but didn't move forward.

'It's not moving!' he cried.

'Handbrake!' said Rachel, leaning in to the front. She unfastened the handbrake and pushed it down, causing the car to burst forward. There was a thud on the roof of the car as Thump rolled off and into the road. Grork veered to the right and picked up the pace. The car was moving quickly but the massive creature was still closing in.

The car engine was loud and strained and was struggling to gain more speed. Simon steered the car right around the outside of the village green.

'Change gear!' yelled Rachel above the sound of the engine.

'How?' Simon shouted back.

'Press the clutch pedal again!'

Simon pressed the pedal with his left foot and Rachel threw the gear stick into second gear. The engine softened slightly but it was still roaring loudly.

'Again!'

Simon pushed the pedal and Rachel pushed the gear stick again. The sound died down and they could finally hear something other than the drone of the engine.

They could hear Grork's footsteps as he neared.

'Faster!' said Jonathon.

Simon jammed his foot down on the accelerator pedal and they picked up speed. Grork roared as the car pulled away, and slammed the ground hard in frustration.

'He's stopped!' said Jonathon.

'Nice driving,' said Ryan.

'Now what?' said Simon. 'Where shall I go?'

'The woods,' said Ryan.

'No,' said Rachel. 'Go to Clayton; we can get help.'

'Yeah,' said Ryan.

Simon knew the way to Clayton, which was only a few miles away from Hedgely, so he turned into the road which led out of the village.

A car smashed into the road ahead and erupted in flames. Simon slammed on the brakes and came within inches of crashing into the wreck.

In the rear view mirror Simon could just make out Grork as he lifted another car above his head and hurled it toward them.

'Reverse!' yelled Jonathon.

Simon didn't need to be asked twice. He slammed the clutch down and Rachel banged the gearstick into reverse gear. The car screeched back, the tyres smoking as they spun on the tarmac. The stench of burnt rubber instantly filled the car, but none of them cared as the car crunched down on the road in the space where they had just been.

They threw the gear back into first and screeched around the village green again. Grork snatched another car and skimmed it across the grass. It bounced twice and flicked up, narrowly missing them as Simon veered to the left. The car slammed onto Mrs Mellor's roof, and one side of the building collapsed into a smoking heap.

'Why is he still throwing cars!' yelled Jonathon.

Grork grabbed another car and launched it across the village green. Simon discovered it was very difficult to drive while at the same trying to avoid flying cars.

'Turn!' yelled Jonathon.

'Where?' said Simon.

Jonathon grabbed the steering wheel and yanked it around. 'Right!'

The car lurched right and onto the village green. The tyres spat mud into the air as the flying car thudded into the stream.

'Hold on,' said Simon. The car hit the ground hard as the back wheels struggled to cross the water. Ryan bounced up and smacked his head on the roof and fell into his sister's lap.

Simon struggled to keep the car straight on the damp grass. The back of the car slipped out and Simon had to twist the steering wheel the opposite way in a battle to keep it from spinning.

Grork was pacing the street for a suitable car. He chose a black four-wheel drive and he heaved it up above his head. The creature's teeth were showing and he was spitting under the effort of holding the car up.

The back of the car skidded again and Simon held

tight to the steering wheel. He fought to turn it against the skid but it was too far gone and the car spun around. He pressed down on the brakes with all his weight but the slick grass couldn't stop the car from spinning.

Simon closed his eyes and clenched the steering wheel.

'Brace yourselves!' he yelled, a second before the car ploughed into something heavy and stopped dead. There was a second loud crash and the sound of metal crumpling.

Suddenly everything went quiet.

Simon steadied his breathing and allowed himself to slowly open his eyes. The front of the car had crushed like a tin can and the steering wheel was pushed close to Simon's chest. Rachel and Ryan were breathing heavily but, apart from Ryan's knock to the head, they were all okay. Jonathon was staring wide-eyed out of a hole which had appeared in the shattered windscreen.

'What is it?' said Simon.

'It's Grork,' said Jonathon. 'I think he's dead.'

Simon had to bash the car door with his shoulder to open it. Jonathon climbed out over the driver's side and tugged at the rear passenger door with Simon. It opened, but only because it fell from its hinges onto the torn up surface of the village green.

Grork was lying still beneath the black four-wheel

drive car. His skin was a vile mess of oranges, blues and reds.

'Well, that's one down, how many more to go?' said Rachel.

'Hey!' came a frantic voice from behind.

The group all turned and readied their weapons.

'Don't shoot me!' cried Abdul, his hands flying up above his head.

CHAPTER TWENTY-EIGHT

'Don't sneak up on us like that,' said Ryan. He lowered the rifle and sighed. 'I could have shot you.'

'Sorry,' said Abdul. He was breathing heavily, and sweat gave his forehead a shiny finish. 'I saw what happened. That crash was huge. Are you okay?'

Simon nodded on behalf of the group. 'I think so.'

'What's happening with the imaginary friends?' said Abdul.

'It turns out they're not so imaginary,' said Ryan.

'They've gone mental,' said Jonathon. 'Kidnapped everyone in the village, and they're trying to kill us by blowing us up and throwing cars at us.'

'What are you doing here?' asked Simon.

'I didn't know where else to go,' said Abdul. 'I woke up this morning and Kannon was in my house messing the whole place up. It's been wrecked.'

'Why?' said Jonathon. He couldn't stop looking at Grork, and expected the creature to jump up at any second.

'Something about how they've found the perfect place or something, and that they didn't need me anymore. I got out of the house before Mum and Dad saw what had happened.'

'Did the thing follow you?' said Rachel.

Abdul shook his head. 'I don't think so. He'd have caught me by now.'

'Well, come to think of it,' said Ryan, his eyes darting across the village green, 'wasn't Thump trying to kill us a second ago?'

There was silence again in the village. If Thump had still been there they would have known about it by now.

'Maybe we ran him over too?' said Jonathon.

'I don't think we're that lucky,' said Rachel. 'Come on, we need to stick to the plan. Let's go to the woods before more of those things show up.'

***

As the group headed into the woods Simon explained to Abdul everything that had happened – everything from the battle with Grork and Thump to the creatures' plans, which Zam had told them. Abdul had difficulty taking it all in and almost swallowed a fly as he listened with an open mouth.

'So if they were planning on taking over Hedgely then why did they invite me to the Secret Circle? And why Warren and Becky and all the others?'

'Zam didn't tell us,' said Ryan. 'But I bet it's because Hedgely is the best location for them.'

'They were probably looking all over the place to see where would be best to take over,' said Jonathon. 'Zam said there was a Gateway from our world to theirs, so maybe there are loads of other Gateways which lead to different places.'

'Maybe,' said Simon. 'That's why they tried to get Abdul in trouble, so they'd think he was mad if he told anybody about the Secret Circle.'

'They're going to think I'm mad anyway,' huffed Abdul. 'They're going to see the house has been trashed and I've gone missing. They're going to go bonkers.'

'We'll make sure everything is put right,' said Rachel. 'We'll go and get our parents back and then they'll be able to tell your parents what happened.'

'What, so my mum and dad can think that all your parents are crazy as well?' said Abdul.

Abdul was right and nobody could think of anything to say to that.

Simon hadn't been inside the woods during the

daytime for quite some time. It certainly looked different between those trees when light was allowed through them. The ground was littered with oranges and browns, and the tall trunks of the trees didn't seem as ominous when you could see to the top.

'Is it much further?' said Rachel.

'No, it's not far,' said Simon.

'It all looks the same,' said Rachel. 'How can you even tell?'

'I've been walking this way in the dark for weeks,' said Jonathon. 'I suppose doing it in the daytime just seems a lot easier when you can see branches on the ground that you need to step over.'

'Yeah, rather than fall over,' said Ryan.

It didn't take them long to reach the clearing. Simon and Ryan stepped out and circled the burnt remains of the fire. It seemed much smaller with the daylight uncovering the surrounding woodland. After deciding the area was safe they motioned for the others to follow, and they all walked into the Secret Circle.

'This is where you came every night?' said Rachel. She had her nose turned up as she kicked a tree stump.

'It's the only place they would meet with us all,' said Ryan.

'Hemlin always said he felt safest here,' added

Jonathon.

'Why would they feel safe here?' said Abdul. 'It's creepy. I can't believe you came here for so long. I was feeling weird the whole time I was here.'

'Mmh!'

The group stood still and listened.

'Mmff!'

There was a muffled voice coming from somewhere within the trees.

'What's that?' whispered Rachel. 'Is that normal?'

'Of course it's not normal,' said Ryan.

'It's coming from back there,' said Jonathon. He was pointing back to where they had entered the clearing.

'Mmh!'

'Hmmr!'

Another voice, this time with a higher pitch.

'Come on, hurry up,' came a third voice. 'Stop struggling!'

Simon waved his arm frantically. 'Get back, hide,' he breathed.

The group scurried into the trees on the opposite side of the clearing. They kept low and held their breath.

On the other side of the clearing Zam entered the Secret Circle. He was still covered in paint, which highlighted his dark grimace. He was carrying Will over his shoulder.

Will was tied up with the same rope that had tied up the creature.

Behind them was Thump. He had Amie. She was bound with thick grey tape and was wriggling desperately.

Simon felt the urge to leap out from the woods. He didn't know what he would do once he was there; squirting them with a water pistol wouldn't do much good.

Jonathon obviously sensed what Simon was thinking and held him down by his shoulder. Simon used his better judgment and watched.

'You climb up and I'll throw them up to you,' said Zam.

'Will do,' said Thump. He dropped Amie to the dirt and she fell awkwardly on her side. She let out a gentle yelp which Simon couldn't bear to hear.

Thump hobbled to the largest tree on the edge of the Secret Circle, a twisted oak tree which erupted at the top into thick branches and a cloud of tangled twigs. The stumpy creature pulled himself up to a high branch and stood at the edge looking down.

'Toss the first one up,' he said.

Zam let Will slip from his shoulder, but caught him just before he hit the ground and used the momentum to hurl him upward. Will screamed as loud as he could through the gag which had been stuck over his mouth. Thump struggled with the weight but managed to hang on to Will and then roll him into a hole which disappeared into the tree trunk.

Simon hadn't noticed the hole before. Usually the darkness masked the tops of the trees, but it was so deep and wide that Will had been rolled in sideways.

Amie was thrown next. Thump had less trouble catching her and easily rolled her into the opening at the top of the tree.

Zam pulled himself up the tree, using the branches like a ladder. He and Thump then walked into the hole and disappeared from view.

The group within the woods had seen it all, and even after the creatures had gone, none of them could think of anything to say. Simon stood up and, his eyes still locked on the hole at the top of the great oak tree, he stepped back into the Secret Circle.

'So that's where they come from?' said Rachel. 'That's the Gateway between our world and theirs?'

'Must be,' said Ryan.

'So that's where we have to go,' said Simon.

'In there?' spat Jonathon. 'Up that massive tree, are you kidding? That must be the biggest tree in the world.'

'Those *things* have Amie,' said Simon. 'They have your grandma, all our parents, and everybody else in the village. Are you telling me you don't want to try to rescue them because you have to climb a tree?'

Jonathon stuttered. 'No.'

'I didn't think so,' said Simon.

Simon reached up to the lowest branch and was just able to pull himself up. He then used the rest of the branches like a climbing frame and scrambled to the top where he rested on the tree's thickest branch. Just to the side of the branch was the hole. Simon could see nothing but blackness inside.

Ryan was next up the tree, followed by Abdul and Rachel. Jonathon stood at the bottom, his neck craned uncomfortably to look up at them.

'I'll just wait for you all down here,' he said. 'I'll be the lookout.'

'Oh yeah, and what if some imaginary friends turn up?' said Ryan.

'I… err… I don't think that branch could hold all our weight.'

'This tree's probably been here for hundreds of years. I don't think a few kids sitting on it will do it any harm,' said Rachel.

'Err…' Jonathon was desperate to find some words which meant he wouldn't have to climb the tree.

'Your grandma's in there, remember,' said Ryan.

'Fine,' said Jonathon. He let Abdul help pull him up to the lowest branch.

'Now what do we do?' said Rachel.

Simon shrugged. 'We just go in, I suppose.'

Without thinking Simon stepped into the opening in the tree trunk and everything went silent and dark.

Chapter Twenty-Nine

Simon hit the ground hard. At least he had landed on grass; anything harder and he wouldn't have been in any fit state to push himself up into a sitting position.

There was a big sun centred in the bright blue sky. The air was close and a warm breeze reminded Simon of a hot day on a foreign beach.

The grass stretched on for miles. Hills rolled up and down like a roller coaster, and only the occasional tangled tree dotted the lush landscape.

Behind, Simon could see the hole he had fallen from. A white, rocky cliff face rose up higher than any cliff he had ever seen before. It ran straight across the grassland for miles in either direction before curving around on itself. Just above head height was the Gateway to the other world. *His* world. A ladder had been made using sticks and vines, and had clearly been used many times.

Simon stepped out of the way just in time to see Ryan collapse through the Gateway. A moment later Abdul tumbled through and landed awkwardly on Ryan's back.

'Thanks for the soft landing,' said Abdul with a grimace.

'You're welcome,' said Ryan.

They all heard Jonathon before they saw him. His screams went from quiet to ear-splitting within seconds, but it gave Ryan and Abdul enough time to move out of the way.

Jonathon sprawled onto the grassland and lay panting, his eyes flicking about the landscape.

'Where are we?' he said.

'I'm pretty sure it's not Hedgely,' said Simon.

'Jonathon, you might want to move,' said Ryan.

Jonathon had steadied his breathing but still lay stretched on the grass. 'Why?'

Rachel somersaulted as she emerged from the Gateway and landed heavily on top of Jonathon, their noses close to touching. Jonathon's face glowed.

'Hi,' he said.

Rachel pushed herself up onto her feet and looked around. 'So, now where?' she said.

They all exchanged looks. Jonathon shrugged.

'Great.'

'Those things only just came in a few minutes

before we did,' said Ryan. 'I bet they're not far. I'll go up onto that hill and look around.'

Rachel nodded and Ryan set off running toward the nearest grassy mound. His gun bounced against his back and the pellets in his pocket rattled loudly.

'It doesn't look much different from home,' said Rachel.

'I don't remember many cliff faces in Hedgely,' said Abdul.

'I don't mean literally,' said Rachel. 'But the grass, the trees, the sky, the sun. You'd think we were still in England.'

'To be fair, we don't get *much* sun in England,' said Abdul with a smile.

'I guess that's why they can breathe our air and don't melt when they get wet,' said Simon. 'It wouldn't be any good for them if they couldn't do or touch anything.'

Ryan was close to reaching the top of the hill. His pace slowed and he scrambled up the last few feet on his hands. At the top he stood up and scanned the horizon.

'Do you see anything?' called Rachel.

Ryan pointed to the right and jumped on the spot.

'Is it them?'

He held his finger to his lips but thrust out his pointing finger and jumped higher.

Rachel shrugged, but Ryan only jumped more.

'Is it Amie and Will?' she shouted.

The earth shook, and Jonathon had to grab onto the cliff face to steady himself. Ryan had stopped jumping and was pointing his rifle down the opposite side of the hill. He was backing away slowly.

'Ryan, what are you doing?' shouted Rachel.

There was another rumble.

'Err, I don't think you should do that,' said Abdul.

'I think you're right,' said Rachel.

Ryan fired a shot, and the snap of the bullet echoed across the cliff's craggy surface.

Another rumble, this time louder. A boulder split away from the cliff and thumped into the grassland a few feet from the Gateway.

Ryan turned and galloped back down the hill. His arms flailed as he desperately fought to keep his balance.

A huge creature heaved itself up onto the mound and roared. It was the size of an elephant but was built like a scaly gorilla. Its neck was long and thick, and at the end was a crocodilian head with an uneven row of yellow teeth.

'Go!' yelled Rachel, but none of them had to be told. They bolted alongside the cliff face as the ground shuddered under each of the creature's huge bounds.

Ryan veered to the left, but the creature continued

to stride forward after the group. As each of its lumbering feet hit the ground the whole earth shook and more rocks broke away from the cliff. As the rocks rained down Abdul had to dive out of the way, while Jonathon leapt over a large rock which sunk deep into the ground.

The creature roared as it approached. Simon glanced over his shoulder and could see its small black eyes staring straight at him. The jaws were open and thick saliva poured from between its teeth.

'Jonathon, duck!' yelled Simon.

Jonathon fell to the ground and the monster's jaws caught a mouthful of pyjama sleeve, but luckily nothing more. The creature slid to a stop and turned back to face Jonathon, who was still lying face down on the grass.

'What's it doing?' said Jonathon.

'Stay still!' said Simon. He and the others had stopped and were watching as the monster leant down and sniffed Jonathon's hair.

A shot cracked across the grasslands and struck the monster on the front shoulder. It roared and stamped its feet, which gave Jonathon enough time to scramble back to his feet and slip between the creature's legs.

Ryan reloaded his rifle and shot the monster again. It roared as he caught it on its rough, greenish stomach.

'Ryan, it's coming for you, run!' yelled Rachel.

Ryan had been lying flat on a grassy mound. As the creature spotted him he jumped up and ran down the other side.

The monster roared again and strode forward. As the others turned and ran it gained speed and the ground shuddered once again.

A chunk of cliff side shattered as it cracked onto the back of the monster. It howled in pain and tumbled to the ground with another thunderous rumble.

'Quickly,' said Simon. He grabbed Jonathon by the arm and the group followed him to the top of the nearest hill. Ryan was already there urging them up while fumbling to reload the rifle. Simon's legs were aching but he made himself ignore the pain; the creature was already on its feet and had spotted them on the hill.

Simon was first to the top and he had to dig his heel in to stop himself from going further. Instead of the hill curving back down to the grasslands, the ground dropped straight down into another sheer cliff face. Below were more grasslands and endless miles of rolling hills.

'Now where?' said Jonathon.

The monster let out a small growl as it approached.

Ryan shot the creature again and hit it inside its open mouth. It shrieked in pain and stumbled back.

'Do that again,' said Rachel.

Ryan dug his hand into his pocket and brought out a pellet.

The creature stamped its feet and rocks crumbled away from the cliff. The ground felt loose beneath Simon's feet.

'Hurry!' said Abdul.

Ryan jammed the pellet into the gun and snapped it back into place just as the creature charged forward. The earth shook and the cliff crumbled more.

'Shoot!'

Ryan pulled the trigger and hit the creature right in the middle of its big, black eye. It bellowed in pain and bowled over itself.

The group parted and dived to the side, giving the monster just enough room to roll past and tumble over the edge of the cliff.

It took everyone a moment to realise what had happened. A thud somewhere below confirmed that the monster had hit the ground hard.

'Was that a good shot or what?' said Ryan, a broad grin on his sweaty face.

'Lucky, more like,' said Abdul.

'Why was that thing after me?' said Jonathon. 'Do I look like a nice meal to all these things?'

Simon peered over the edge of the cliff. Below, he

could see the monster laying still, a pool of dark blood forming around its head. But it was something else that had caught his attention. It was Hemlin.

'Hey, look,' said Simon. He motioned for the others to look over the grasslands below.

'It's Hemlin!' announced Jonathon.

'Shh,' scorned the others.

Hemlin kicked the monster and shouted something toward the base of the cliff. A moment later Ralcar came into view and jumped onto the back of the dead monster.

'What are they doing?' whispered Abdul.

'It looks like they're talking,' said Ryan.

Hemlin and Ralcar turned their heads up to the cliff top and the group ducked back.

'Did they see us?' said Jonathon.

'I don't think so,' said Simon. 'You guys stay back; I'll have a look.'

Simon slowly peered back over the edge of the cliff and saw that Hemlin and Ralcar were facing each other. Over to the left, two more figures emerged from the cliff base.

It was Thump and Zam. Amie and Will were still draped over their shoulders.

'I think we've found where our parents are being kept,' said Simon.

CHAPTER THIRTY

The group walked along the cliff edge but made sure they kept back. The last thing they wanted was to either slip off the cliff or show themselves to the creatures below.

Amie and Will had been carried away toward the cliff base. Hemlin tied the thick legs of the fallen monster together with rope and then followed the others out of view. Jonathon made a point of frequently checking the open grasslands in case another one decided to reveal itself from behind the many hills.

Simon led the group and examined the cliff top as they walked. He knew there would be a way down somewhere and just ahead, he could see a small nook cut into the ground. As they moved closer it became clear that it was a steep track which curved around and down the cliff face.

The track had been carved into the side of the cliff

face like a groove, but was barely wide or tall enough to stand in. If they were going to try that way then they would certainly need to keep a steady foot.

'I'm not going down there,' said Jonathon.

'There aren't any other ways,' said Simon

'There must be.'

'I don't think these things have invented lifts yet,' said Ryan.

'It's too high,' said Jonathon. 'The tree was one thing, but this is huge. It must be three hundred feet. All you have to do is put one step wrong and you're off.'

'I don't think we have time to look for a nice gentle slope down the cliff side,' snapped Rachel. 'It's either this, or we just go back and live with the monsters in Hedgely. It's up to you.'

'Don't make me choose!'

The ground rumbled and the bulky frame of a second monster bounded out from behind a grassy mound. It spotted the group and roared.

'Me first!' yelped Jonathon.

He shoved past Simon and pushed his back against the cliff. The track was thin and the ends of Jonathon's shoes poked out over the edge. He sidestepped slowly down the track.

Above, the creature ran toward them.

Abdul was next to sidle across the cliff face, followed closely by Rachel, who had the backpack with the dynamite hooked over her arm. She was taller than the others so she had to bend down to avoid her hair dragging along the top of the groove.

Ahead, Jonathon stumbled and clung tightly to a vine which stuck out from the rocks.

'Hurry!' yelled Ryan as he held on to the track face first. The creature was close now and Simon had no room on the track to move into.

'Jonathon! Move!' cried Rachel. Jonathon was staring at the ground below and his knees were knocking together. With a gentle nudge from Abdul, he moved down the track and the others followed, giving Simon just enough room to step on and out of the way of the monster.

The beast roared. It pounded the ground with its massive legs, and rocks broke away from the cliff face. Ryan cried out as the rock he was using to hold on to crumbled, but Abdul managed to use his shoulder to stop him from falling back.

'You need to keep moving, Jonathon,' said Simon. The monster was snapping its jaws over the edge of the cliff. If Simon had reached out his hand he would have been able to touch it. Its breath was hot and sickly.

'With every step you make you'll be closer to the

ground,' said Rachel.

'With every step I make I'm closer to falling,' said Jonathon.

'With every step you don't make I'm closer to being eaten!' yelled Simon. 'For goodness' sake, move!'

Jonathon sidled down the cliff face with the others close behind. As Simon moved away the monster lost interest and its crunching, dripping jaws disappeared back above the cliff top.

It felt like they were on the track for hours. With each small stumble or slip their hearts would pound faster and their stomachs leapt into their throats. Jonathon moaned the whole time, while the others moaned about Jonathon.

As they neared the bottom, Simon could just see the monster that had fallen from the cliff. Its legs and jaws had been bound tightly and the grass around its body had been stained red. It definitely looked dead.

Once his feet touched down on the grass Jonathon punched the air. As Simon joined him he punched Jonathon in the shoulder.

'Thanks for that, I was nearly eaten then.'

The group took a break at the base of the cliff to steady their hearts and rest their legs. Looking back up the track Simon found it hard to believe they had all just descended such a treacherous pathway.

'GET OFF!'

The voice had come from somewhere along the cliff base.

'Who was that?' said Abdul.

'It sounded like Mum,' said Ryan.

Rachel's shoulders sank back in agreement.

'Then this is it,' said Simon. 'This is where it either all goes right, or all goes wrong.'

'Everything always goes wrong for me,' said Jonathon.

'I'm starting to wish we'd left you at the tree,' said Ryan.

'I do wish I'd been left at the tree!'

'Oh, well, why don't you just wander back up the mountain and try and outrun that… thing?'

'Maybe I should.'

'NO!' came another terrified voice. It sounded like Will.

'You boys can finish this later,' said Rachel, 'but I'm going to go and do what I can in there. If you want to try and save our parents then come with me.'

Rachel, Simon, Ryan and Abdul stuck close to the cliff face and moved toward where the sounds had come from. Jonathon kicked the ground and dug his hands into his pyjama pockets.

The banana was still there, albeit bruised and squashed.

Jonathon huffed as his thoughts turned to his grandma. He could hear the shouts coming from further down the cliff, and an image formed in his head of his grandma being the one shouting.

Jonathon shoved the banana back into his pocket and ran to catch up with the others. He'd be there to make sure his grandma peeled his banana for him.

Chapter Thirty-One

The group only had to walk a hundred feet along the bottom of the cliff until they reached the entrance to a cave. It wasn't a large opening – around the size of a small car. Deep in the darkness was an orange glow which dully lit the craggy walls, and somewhere inside was quiet chatter and the scurrying of footsteps.

'Ryan, are you loaded?' asked Rachel.

Ryan nodded.

'Abdul, take these.' Rachel handed Abdul the backpack with the dynamite and pushed the lighter into his hand. 'Keep them separate; we don't want them going off in your hand.'

Abdul nodded and slipped the lighter into his pocket.

'Jonathon, you stay out here and keep watch.'

Jonathon smiled.

'If you hear or see anything, shout as loud as you can, okay?'

'I can do that,' said Jonathon.

A scream echoed through the cave, followed by a chorus of gasps and cries.

Rachel stepped in to the cave. 'Follow me.'

***

The deeper they moved into the cave, the less the sunlight lit their path. The orange glow gave the damp walls a look of warmth, but there was a noticeable coolness in the air compared to outside the cave.

The cave curved around to the right and the walls closed in. Simon and the others stepped lightly. Somewhere ahead they could hear the sound of movement; it didn't take much for sound to bounce around the cave.

'Don't you dare!'

It was a woman's voice, and it was close. Simon's heart flipped as he recognised it.

It was his mum. At least she was still alive.

'There's not much we wouldn't dare do. Keep quiet.'

It sounded like Kannon. There was a dull thud and the sound of people gasping.

'Don't hit my wife,' said the voice Simon recognised

as his dad's.

'Your whole family are feisty, aren't they?' said Kannon. 'Such a respectable quality. But I did warn you to keep quiet.'

There was another thud followed by something heavy falling to the cave floor. Somebody started whimpering and sniffing loudly.

Simon was sure it was Amie.

The orange glow grew brighter as the cave turned a sharp left corner. Simon motioned for the group to stick tight to the wall. He knew the creatures and their parents were just there. He could hear the sound of the victims' sobs and the scurrying of the imaginary friends as they moved around the cave.

'Abdul, pass me one of those,' said Simon. Abdul passed him one of the four remaining sticks of dynamite from the backpack and handed him the lighter.

'Are you all ready?' he said.

There were nods around the group.

Simon took a deep breath, ignored the pounding of his heart, and stepped around the corner.

The cave opened up into a wide open cavern. Stalactites hung down from the ceiling while stalagmites clawed up from the rocky floor. Flickering torches lined the walls and cast dancing streaks of orange across the damp rock. The cave rose up in levels, with each level full of wooden boxes and sacks packed with various knick-knacks. There were dozens of creatures scurrying around; some were carrying crates while others stood talking in groups.

To the right was a large cage made from wood. It was tied together with strong rope and the gaps between them were wide enough for Simon to see through.

Inside the cage were the adults from Hedgely.

'Well, look who has saved us the trouble of fetching them here,' said Kannon with a sly smile.

Simon held the stick of dynamite above his head. 'Come any closer and I'll blow everything in here to pieces,' he announced.

***

Outside, Jonathon was already bored. He could hear muffled sounds from within the cave, but it wasn't clear enough so he could tell what was going on.

Jonathon strolled over to the dead animal, which had its thick legs bound together with rope. He touched its rough, grey skin and something inside it gurgled.

***

'What do you plan on doing, Simon?' asked Kannon in a calm voice.

'Whatever I have to,' said Simon. His voice wasn't as calm.

The creatures around the cave had all stopped what they were doing. Every eye in the cave was focused on Simon and the dynamite.

'Simon, what are you doing?' said Helen from inside the cage. 'Get out of here.'

'It's too late for that,' snapped Kannon. 'You'll just have to die at the same time as everybody else now.'

'Pity,' said Hemlin, who had appeared beside Kannon. 'I was looking forward to watching them all work their fingers bloody.'

'Let our parents go,' said Simon.

***

Jonathon stepped back from the creature. The gurgle he had heard must have just been the effects of its body shutting down.

'Stupid monster,' said Jonathon. He kicked the creature's hoofed foot.

***

Chuckles echoed through the cave.

'I have to give you credit,' said Kannon. 'You certainly have guts. More than the rest of them. All of you have just rolled over and died. If more of you were like him, then maybe we'd have had more work to do. So for that, I thank you.'

Simon took the lighter from his pocket and held it for Kannon to see.

'So you have a little bomb, big deal. One of those little things might have given Zam a bit of a headache, but it's not going to do much to all of us, is it?'

'We have more,' blurted Simon.

'And then what? You'd better have a thousand of them. Otherwise, you just keep making everything easier for us.'

***

Jonathon smiled and kicked the monster again. It certainly made him feel better about being chased by it earlier.

'Stupid fat idiot!' he said and kicked it again.

The creature opened its eyes.

Chapter Thirty-Two

'What are you waiting for?' said Kannon loudly.

'For you to let our parents go,' Simon said.

'I thought I'd made it clear that that wasn't an option.'

Simon flicked the lighter and a small flame appeared.

'Go on then, get it over and done with,' said Kannon smugly.

'Last chance,' said Simon.

'Do your worst.'

'Simon!'

It was Jonathon from the cave entrance.

'Ahh, is that the fat one?' said Hemlin.

'You really have done us a big favour, bringing everybody here,' said Kannon.

'Simon! Rachel!' Jonathon sounded frantic.

Simon kept his eyes on Kannon. 'Jonathon, what is it?' he shouted.

Jonathon burst into the cave. Even the sight of the creatures didn't make him drop his pace.

'Run!' he yelped.

The piercing roar of a monster filled the cave. The ground shook and rocks rained from the ceiling.

Kannon's smile dropped and he turned to run.

The monster ploughed through the cave wall and bellowed in triumph. Jonathon bolted to the back of the cavern and the monster gave chase, swinging its bulky head to one side to bat one of the helpless creatures out of its path.

'Everybody run!' cried Rachel.

The group turned and dashed toward the exit of the cave.

All except Simon, who was watching the monster scramble desperately after Jonathon.

'Kill it!' screamed Kannon. 'Go for the legs!'

A small group of the creatures was slashing at the monster, but it swung its head down and easily swatted them to one side like they were merely flies.

The monster stopped. It raised its head high and sniffed the air.

Simon ran over to the cage and hugged his mum

through the wooden bars.

'You're so silly for coming here,' she said.

'What were you thinking?' said his dad.

'Somebody had to do something,' said Simon. 'Everybody get back.'

Simon lit the dynamite and threw it into the empty corner of the cage. With a loud crack it exploded and wood splintered and scattered over the cave floor.

'Everybody run!' yelled Simon. Bodies poured from the cage and scurried over to the exit. 'Jonathon, keep that thing over there!'

'I don't want to keep it over here!' yelped Jonathon, who was hiding behind a leather sack.

From the ledge above, one of the creatures tossed down a net which draped over the monster's head. It roared and thrashed back and forth, but gave Jonathon enough time to scurry from his hiding place and over to where Simon was leading the last few adults from the cage.

'What did you do?' said Simon.

Jonathon gasped for breath. 'I just kicked it, that's all.'

'Why would you do that?'

'I don't know!'

Hemlin appeared in front of them. He was baring every one of his needle-sharp teeth. 'You!'

'I'm sorry,' said Jonathon.

'You've been nothing but a nuisance for me,' spat the creature. 'I've had to listen to your annoying laughter and put up with your stupidity for weeks! If nothing else, I want to take pleasure in killing you myself.'

Jonathon whimpered and stepped back. He fumbled in his pockets for something, *anything*, which he could use as a weapon.

He pulled out a squashed banana. He sighed, but threw it at Hemlin anyway, and mushy banana smeared over the creature's chest.

'My point is proven,' said Hemlin.

The monster roared and tore through the net with its powerful jaws. It spotted Jonathon and bound towards him.

'Or I could let the Hoarok do it,' said Hemlin, who then vanished right in front of them.

Jonathon and Simon didn't run; they had nowhere to go. To their right was the empty cage and behind them and to the left was the craggy cave wall.

The monster approached. Its teeth dripped with thick saliva.

Suddenly it stopped and sniffed the air. Then with one snap of its massive jaws it grabbed a blood-soaked Hemlin and thrashed him from side to side. The imaginary friend could barely manage to scream before his body went limp.

'What's happening?' yelled Jonathon.

Simon saw the banana peel by their feet.

'It must be the banana,' said Simon. He bent down and grabbed the mushy banana peel and flung it over the monster's head. It landed with a slap on a higher ledge, and the monster scrambled and roared in frustration as it tried to snatch it in its huge jaws.

'Go!'

It only took them a moment to emerge in the bright sunlight. Simon could see the residents of Hedgely already edging along the thin track which cut through the cliff face. Some were weeping and screaming, but they moved quickly, and the leaders were almost at the top.

Simon gave Jonathon a leg up onto the walkway, and they followed. Somewhere underground the creature was still bounding and roaring; every time it did a rock would slip from the cliff face and someone would scream.

'Jonathon, hurry!' yelled Simon.

'I'm going as fast as I can!'

'You need to go faster.'

The rumbling from underground stopped, which drew attention to the otherwise silent world around them.

'There they are!' came a rasping voice from below.

Simon could see Kannon on the grasslands. He was surrounded by bloodied and battered creatures, all of which had their eyes narrowed and their teeth on show.

'Kill them,' ordered Kannon.

Three of the imaginary friends began climbing the rocky cliff while the others headed for the track. They were obviously more skilled at walking up it, as they gained ground very quickly.

'Jonathon!' snapped Simon.

Jonathon's mouth hung open. He had stopped moving and was watching the creatures approach.

'They're nearly here, move!'

Simon nudged Jonathon and he sidled up the cliff face. His eyes were clamped shut and, with each step, he let out a small whimper.

The others were already at the top of the cliff, leaving just the two of them still climbing. Abdul and Ryan hurled rocks down at the creatures which were climbing the vertical face but, other than crumble as they smacked into their shoulders, they didn't stop the creatures from pursuing.

'Hurry,' said Rachel from the top. 'Not far to go, Jonathon, but you have to hurry because they're right behind you.'

Jonathon opened his eyes and look past Simon. The creatures were close.

Jonathon picked up his pace and almost slipped as he practically hopped to the top of the track.

Simon felt relief wash over him as Jonathon's foot disappeared over the top of the cliff. He readied himself, took a deep breath, and reached up to pull himself over.

'I don't think so!' said a harsh voice. A bony hand wrapped around Simon's ankle and his balance gave way. Simon tipped forward and he swung his arms behind, grabbing at anything his fingers could grasp.

'Get off!' yelled Simon. He wrapped his arm around a root which wormed out from the rock face. The nearest imaginary friend had latched on to his leg and the others behind were reaching around and swiping their arms. Each of them had a look of sick pleasure on their faces as Simon kicked out his legs.

The root began to pull from the cliff face and Simon jarred forward. He managed to kick the nearest creature in the jaw with his free foot, and it stumbled back into the others.

'Simon!'

Simon looked around. He'd heard his dad.

'Look up!'

Brian was reaching down over the edge of the cliff, his hand outstretched toward Simon's arm.

'Reach up to me!'

209

Simon swung his arm up but missed. The creatures were back on their feet and were edging back toward him.

'Try again.'

Simon swung again and missed by an inch.

'Come on, Simon.'

The creatures flailed their arms and latched on to Simon's legs. Simon kicked out and struck one on the shoulder, using the blow to push himself up and grab on to his dad's hand.

'Hold on,' said Brian. He pulled Simon up, a creature still clinging to his legs and, with one hard stamp, Simon broke its nose and sent it plummeting to the bottom of the cliff.

Abdul and Ryan threw their last rock and turned to Simon and Brian.

'They're at the top,' said Abdul. 'Run.'

They set off running to join the others. The villagers were already making their way across the rolling hills of the grasslands. The children led the way while the older generation struggled to keep a swift pace. It didn't take Simon and the others long to catch up to them.

Some of the imaginary friends were closing in as more poured over the cliff's edge and broke into a gallop.

Jonathon looked over his shoulder and yelped. Simon had never seen him run so fast.

Suddenly the floor rumbled and a familiar roar echoed across the grasslands.

An enormous monster, another one of the Hoarok beasts, bounded up from behind a grass mound and peered at the stampeding people and imaginary friends. It sniffed the air, and saliva dripped from its massive crocodilian jaws.

Jonathon seemed to pick up speed again.

The monster roared and bounded forward. The stream of imaginary friends veered to the side to avoid the creature's bulk, but it ploughed through them and crushed a few unlucky ones beneath its feet.

Those who avoided the monster's feet ran alongside it in pursuit of the villagers. Any who came too close were batted to the side with one harsh swipe of its head.

Abdul swerved toward Simon and held out the bag.

'Do you have the lighter?' Abdul said between heavy breaths.

Simon dug his hand into his pocket.

'Here,' he rasped.

'I have three sticks of dynamite left; throw it to me and I'll finish that thing off.'

Simon passed Abdul the lighter like a baton and they parted ways.

Abdul took the first stick from the bag and lit it. He held tight to it for a moment, then dropped it just behind.

Abdul didn't look back, but Simon glanced over his shoulder at just the right time to see the dynamite explode. Grass and dirt burst up and one of the imaginary friends fell into a bloodied heap beside the crater it created. The monster and the other imaginary friends were still closing in.

'It missed,' said Simon. 'Do it a little to the right.'

Abdul lit the second stick. He let it sizzle in his hand, then dropped it again and saw it nestle in a clump of tangled weeds.

The dynamite exploded and rained clumps of dirt down onto the grasslands. The monster bellowed and shook its head as its foot sunk into the crater. Its body twisted and it tried to steady itself, but it rolled over to the side and crushed a group of approaching imaginary friends.

'Got it!' yelled Simon.

But the imaginary friends didn't stop. They simply clambered over the flailing creature as it struggled to free its foot from the hole.

Ahead Simon could see the villagers climbing into the Gateway. They were piling through like mice scurrying into a burrow, while the more fragile residents had to be pushed, pulled and almost thrown through.

Simon saw Amie and his mum enter the Gateway. His dad was also there and was helping Jonathon's grandma up the rickety ladder.

Behind, Simon could hear the footsteps of the approaching creatures, but he dared not look back – the Gateway was only a few feet away.

Rachel leapt through the Gateway, followed closely by Ryan and Abdul. Simon heaved Jonathon through next, who tumbled through with a yelp.

Now all that was left was Simon and Brian.

'You first, son,' said Brian.

Simon thought about arguing, but when he saw how close the imaginary friends were he let his dad lift him onto the ledge of the Gateway. Simon turned and held out his hand. His dad grabbed on and pulled himself up, and the two of them tumbled backwards until everything went black.

CHAPTER THIRTY-THREE

Simon opened his eyes and saw the evening sky framed by tangled tree branches. He pushed himself onto his elbows and saw the tree he had fallen from.

Rachel reached out and offered her hand.

'We did it,' she said. 'A few bumps and sore heads, but we're all here.'

Most of Hedgely's residents were already heading through the trees back to the village but those who remained were rubbing their backs or tending to cuts and scrapes. Simon saw his mum and dad cuddling Amie, who was quietly stifling her tears.

'Why are they not following us?' said Ryan, his eyes fixed on the tree.

'I don't know,' said Rachel. 'Because we know about them, maybe. We won.'

'They've given up easily, haven't they?' said Simon.

Somewhere a scream rang through the trees and everybody stood in silence.

Simon jogged over to Abdul. 'Do you have the last piece of dynamite?'

Abdul held up the bag and Simon took the bomb. He ran over to the Gateway tree and pushed it into a hole within the knotted bark.

'I need the lighter,' Simon shouted.

A pain-filled scream prevented Abdul from replying, and the bloodied body of an imaginary friend flew through the Gateway and landed hard on the clearing floor.

'Quickly!'

Two more imaginary friends burst through the Gateway and as their blood-soaked, bruised bodies landed they grunted and gurgled in pain.

But nobody paid any attention to the imaginary friends when the battered, shrieking head of the Hoarok monster snaked in through the Gateway. It thrashed around and screamed so loudly that Simon had to cover his ears. The trees around the clearing shook like they were in an earthquake and the snap of the monsters jaws was hard to tell apart from the crunch of the breaking branches.

'Everybody keep back,' yelled Brian. He had led Helen and Amie to the back of the clearing and was beckoning his son.

Simon stared at the monster. It swiped its head to one side and splintered the largest branch of the Gateway tree. The branch fell hard on the ground and just missed one of the writhing imaginary friends.

'Abdul, the lighter!' yelled Simon.

Abdul tossed the lighter across the clearing. As Simon reached out his open hand something clasped his leg and he was dragged to the ground.

The imaginary friend pulled Simon closer and snarled. It bit his leg hard, and Simon cried out in pain. He kicked at the creature's head with his free foot, but it didn't release its locked grip.

The creature continued bellowing and thrashing. Branches fell like rain all around the clearing and Ryan was hit hard on the shoulder.

The second imaginary friend had climbed to its feet and had latched itself onto Jonathon's back. Rachel screeched and thumped it in the neck, but the creature held on and hissed.

Abdul grabbed a fallen branch and swung it over Simon's head. The imaginary friend groaned as the wood splintered over its back, which gave Simon enough time to pull his leg free and snatch the lighter from the dirt.

The monster swiped its head down again. Simon dived to the side and reached the base of the Gateway tree.

He flicked the top of the lighter and the flame jumped to life. Abdul ran over to Jonathon and helped to beat the creature from his back while the other still rolled around in pain on the ground.

'Do it, Simon!' yelled Brian.

Simon didn't need to be asked twice. He moved the flame to the fuse of the dynamite and within a second it began to fizz.

'Run!'

Simon bolted from the base of the tree and joined his parents at the edge of the clearing. The monster was relentless; its screams and snapping jaws even drowned out the sound of Jonathon's squeals.

But when the dynamite exploded, the monster stopped.

Chips of wood littered the clearing. The tree groaned and creaked as it struggled to keep itself upright under the strain of the hole which was now blown into its side.

The group backed into the cover of the woods as the tree began to twist and topple towards them. Even the imaginary friend stopped its struggle; its glassy eyes were locked on the monster as the tree collapsed. The monster bellowed again and desperately tried to pull its head back through the Gateway.

But it was too late. As the tree thundered into the ground the monster's neck snapped like the surrounding branches and it didn't make another sound.

While they stood in shock as the fallen tree settled, the imaginary friend released its grip from Jonathon and darted into the woods.

CHAPTER THIRTY-FOUR

Hedgely was never the same after the attack by the imaginary friends. On returning from the woods beaten and bloodied, the residents called an emergency meeting in the village hall to discuss what they should do.

'Let's go to the papers!' shrieked one woman.

'And have reporters prowling around the area? I don't think so,' said another.

'We need to keep this secret,' said somebody else. 'If we tell anybody about this they'll send us all to the nuthouse and tear the village down.'

'But what if these things are appearing elsewhere in the country? We need to warn them.'

'If this had happened elsewhere I doubt they'd have been as lucky as we were. We would have heard something by now.'

'Are we all in agreement? We will keep this solely

within the village and will not discuss it with anybody who isn't present today?'

There were mutterings of approval around the hall.

**

The following morning some of the men from Hedgely ventured back into the woods with freshly-sharpened axes. On their return, over two hours later, they reported that they had successfully chopped the Gateway tree into tiny chips.

They also reported that the monster's head was missing from the Gateway. At least, they said, there were no signs that other imaginary friends had come through.

**

Abdul returned home to find police searching his house. His parents had called the police to report a break-in and hadn't even realised their son was missing until he didn't come home for dinner that evening. He was grounded for a month, but that was fine. At least they didn't know about the imaginary friends.

**

Nobody had seen any sign of the imaginary friend which had managed to escape. The villagers of Hedgely would often talk about it and come up with wild theories that it was still living amongst them.

Others thought it would live out its days in the woods, looking for a way home. Because of that, the children of the village were banned from ever stepping into the trees again.

***

Will had to explain to his parents why there was a crater in the living room floor. His parents were quite understanding, but he was asked never to do it again.

Jonathon had decided from then on he was going to peel his own bananas in the morning, but his grandma would still iron his socks and pour him his orange juice. On Tuesday they all returned to school and spoke nothing of the Secret Circle.

***

Brian and Helen took a few days off work and spent the time with Simon and Amie. After school they would pick them up and go for a meal, mainly as an apology and a thank you to

221

Simon, but of course also for Amie for being so brave. Once home, Simon would play games with Brian while Helen tucked Amie into bed.

Once Simon headed to bed himself, he nestled deep into the warmth of his covers. His leg still hurt but the bite mark had started to fade, and his bruises no longer ached.

Simon closed his eyes and drifted to sleep. He wasn't kept awake by the sound of his sister talking any more.

Acknowledgements

The imaginary friends have been with me for the best part of five years up until the release of this book, and I would like to thank everybody who has influenced and supported me along the way. Thank you Verity for your superb artwork and thank you to Justin, Rachael and Denise for your English language skills. My parents, my friends and of course Gracie, you all help me to achieve my goals in so many ways. Thank you.

ABOUT THE AUTHOR

Mike is a writer, film maker, videographer and all round strange guy. He enjoys making people laugh, riding roller coasters and writing in the third person.

You can find him on Twitter **@TheOnlyMikeJ**, and his lovely website at **www.mikejeavons.com**

7679837R00136

Printed in Great Britain
by Amazon.co.uk, Ltd.,
Marston Gate.